# Next Year In Jerusalem

Rosy Cole

Header quotations: *William Blake*

ISBN 978-0-9556877-4-7

New Eve Publishing
Great Britain

"All that time, life kept putting its face around the door, but never came into the room."

When Angel learnt her days were numbered, she viewed a frosted landscape that chilled more than blood and bone. To tell Jude would put a false complexion on their life together. Immersed in the precarious expansion of his business, he little suspected the true cause of her failing health and changed outlook.

Events were only too ready to conspire in her silence. The dilemma swiftly wove its web of misunderstanding which prompted Jude's infidelity and Angel's poignant rapport with 'the bookseller of Glenfinnie', reaching a crisis where Jude's own life was imperilled.

While she fought shy of the truth, Angel couldn't know how, on the other side of fear, an incorruptible world would awaken within her and turn shadows to blessings.

She was to make an inner journey of discovery, seeing in her condition some analogy with the global unrest of our times.

This is a story which prompts haunting reflection on the mystical nature of human 'presence'.

Were Life and Death two sides of the same coin?

# Daybreak

*For I dance*
*And drink and sing,*
*Till some blind hand*
*Shall brush my wing.*

# Daybreak

My name is Angel. Angel Brightman since I married Jude. Before that, I was known as Angel St. Clare. A nun found me on the Convent doorstep when I was a few days old. I think I was born on a Friday, a day of Sorrowful Mysteries.

The nun must have thought I was a cherub sent from heaven! The Poor Clares are a Franciscan Order, committed to poverty, purity and prayer, whose measured days are bathed in peace and doubt-defying light, sobriety and song, and sprinkled with a modicum of mirth, so that my earliest encounters with humanity were of an impartial devotion. They moved about the shadows like seraphs in sackcloth whose wings and transfigured robes were yet unjustified, making the beginning of the journey seem so much like the end.

My mother – she must have loved me! – I sometimes sense a yearning presence and think I glimpse her angst-ridden brow – left me well-packaged in a clean nightie and shawl, with extra clothes and a tin of powdered baby milk. She sent me on my way as well set up as she knew how. I dare say she didn't possess the moral and social means to keep me. Perhaps no one else knew of my birth and she would be forever racked by her guilty secret, wondering how I'd turned out and what sort of human being *she* really was.

There was, I have learned, a flurry of publicity in the local press, but no one came forward to claim me. In due course, I was sent to St. Mary's Orphanage to be cared for there, where, from the dawn of memory, I was encouraged to look upon Our Lady as my mother, to say the Rosary with diligence and to pray to her Son through her mediation. We were taught to feel that we were privileged to have been *found*, to have fetched up from the belly of Jonah on the shores of Holy Island.

The events of those infant years are a blur, uncomplicated by nostalgia. I was neither happy nor unhappy, but suspended in a sort of limbo betwixt and between, eternally expectant. It was as good a school for actual life as any, I suppose, and no doubt for me, better than most as things turned out. Our day is shorter than we think.

Only a few incidents from that era are clearly defined. One, in particular, is rendered more starkly than the rest...

Snow fell unexpectedly in my hopeful seventh spring. It made shadows of the bare boughs. It sent shivers down the spindly spine of young birch. It found out the eroded pointing in the brickwork. With a gentle insistence it gathered along the window-ledges, made portholes of the panes and silenced the astonished birds. Flake by flake, it settled upon the lawns Simms had already mown twice that season, and obliterated the paths as though it meant business. Soon it had created a ghostly monochrome world. A child's world.

No one guessed it was coming. The weather forecast had been promising. It came without warning, this taste of winter in May; a thief in the night.

Mrs Simms, housekeeper at St. Mary's declared: "Well, well, I never! That's put paid to the picnic, then. Nipped our plans right in the bud, that has, dear." She liked things to be orderly, predictable.

"Never mind, I suspect the children won't be too disappointed," Sister Joseph said in a pleasant rallying tone. "They'll be just as happy making snowmen as picking cowslips. You can't order the weather, I'm afraid."

She was right. We whooped with delight and scrambled on to the sills to watch the sky come tumbling down to earth at last. We had longed for snow and felt cheated. Unlike its predecessor, the winter had been a sequence of lethargic days, of damp pavements and mild winds that never got off the ground. There was no cutting edge to it. No blade-bright December or January to sting colour into your cheeks and pinch your toes. Spring came unheralded, robbed of its magic. Even the snowdrops flowered unremarked.

But the advent of snow put a new complexion on things. It lent poignancy to the frail evidence of rebirth.

Throughout lunch that day, which included mortifying wads of bread-and-butter pudding I shall never forget, we agitated to be let loose on the sugar-frosted landscape and, as soon as it was over, crowded the exit noisily. We rolled in the snow, scooped it up and stuffed it by the fistful into our mouths, tobogganed in the dell where the oaks were strung with rubber tyres. Long earthen scars appeared upon its slopes. The air was thick with shrieks of glee and icy missiles exploding on ducked backs. Some built a fortress in the shrubbery, irrigating its mote with a length of hose burgled from Simms' shed, until the brindled snow had turned to slush, the towers sank in ruins and the ramparts were no more.

"I know," cried someone, "let's dig for buried treasure!"

And as enthusiasm quickened among us, we fell to seeking our fortune in the swede patch Simms had painstakingly prepared for the new crop. The primary colours of our spades struck a contrast with the snow and with the cheerless garments thrust upon us in those years of rationing after another fullscale war. The world had not entirely awakened to its own survival.

Fortunately, Simms had gone into town on an errand for Matron, and was not around to see his beloved domain turned inside out, soil and snow and clods of clay flying from the trench. The going was tough. The purposeful were soon singled out from those in search of aimless distraction.

"The ground is hard," complained the whey-faced Polish boy Matron fed with iron pills and spoons of loathsome fish-oil he spat out at her. "I try somewhere else."

A groan went up from the rest of us. We knew him of old.

"Novak's chickened out before we've started," sniffed Thomas in disgust, a good-natured elderly boy of eleven who took command of all our enterprises.

"It's all right for you, my spade's too blunt," the quarrelsome Lucy told him.

"Mine's broken," wailed little Humphrey, and the corners of his mouth curved down and the beads of moisture in the corners of his eyes filled out.

"Have mine, then," I said. I was dizzy and my chest felt sore.

"You're my best friend," he beamed up at me. "You can have my pudding tomorrow. Unless it's treacle tart!"

"Old Beaky says she's got a dicky ticker," Thomas informed them, mopping his overheated brow upon his sleeve. "Reckon he could be right. She's always out of breath."

Frustratingly, my eagerness for adventure was no measure of my ability to keep pace with the high spirits of the rest. Dr. Jennings had forbidden me to dance. At Christmas, I danced solo in the pantomime we put on for our patrons and almsgivers and a lady from the audience was so taken with my performance she offered to arrange proper tuition. Nadia, her name was, a gamin creature in red fox fur up to her ears, a real ballerina, Reverend Mother had emphasised, and a member of the

Rambert company. "Such an honour, Angel. You are blessed."

It was a fairytale come true. Little had I thought to become what I most longed to be! Undaunted by the discipline, I practised my steps morning and night. Madame Minoret at the ballet school was amazed by my progress. A natural, she had confirmed to Nadia, an empathetic dancer, whatever that meant. And Nadia had twinkled. "We shall see what we shall see," she said.

But Dr. Jennings had come along and put a cold stopper upon my ribs and squinted down his aquiline nose and warned that the dancing must cease. All strenuous activity was to be avoided.

"A slight heart murmur," he confided to Sister Agnes, relaxing his stethoscope. "Nothing to be unduly concerned about at this stage. However, we had better play safe. Eh, young lady?"

During the night, I went down with a fever. Dr. Jennings was summoned and diagnosed a severe attack of 'flu. Alarm grew when I failed to respond to treatment. For two days and nights my condition did not abate and even in delirium my toes formed points under the covers. On the third day, the crisis passed. I surfaced, clearer-eyed, to a new world of textures, tastes and sounds. The acuity of my perception was startling. It was as though I had been recast in another mould. The calm relationship of objects, after the storm which had imparted a sinister meaning to them, moved within me a remote happiness. I found myself in the sick bay, in a large bed high off the disinfected linoleum, with Felicity Rag-Doll ailing beside me and a painted Tau Cross on one wall and the Sacred Heart of Jesus on another, inflamed and bleeding, and the Michelangelo Pietà on a third. Down the corridor, Mildred Semple was practising her piano pieces. I sat up and flung the blankets aside. But the second the floor touched cold to my foot, I remembered. How I pined for my lost freedom! It was torture not to be able to take flight and dance, like being a bird and having your wings clipped.

Life was never the same again. All I did involved undue effort. I tried not to give in but tired quickly. What I hated most of all was being left behind like the lame boy in *The Pied Piper of Hamelin*, forever shut out of the enchanted kingdom inside the mountain because he couldn't keep pace.

In the garden, I looked on dispirited, while the hole dilated at my feet and my companions alighted on the rewards of their industry. Several blue glass beads were found, an old clay pipe, its bowl still intact, a tortoiseshell comb and a bun penny. As the afternoon wore on, we lost all track of time and place until we heard Sister Agnes calling us across the snow.

Thomas hitched his spectacles up to the bridge of his nose with his forefinger and consulted the position of the sun. "Right men! Pocket the booty! It's a long trek back to base. Look lively, Novak, or you'll be spending the night in an eighteen foot drift. Wolf-fodder, that's what you'll be!"

We followed him, our Wellington boots cutting a swathe through the smudged lawn. Already the snow on the terrace had melted. A thrush sang in the apple tree stippled with green. The conservatory threw back a pale sky splashed with flame. It was warm. The air smelled of spring and of picnics postponed, of an outing to the sea if we were lucky. Tomorrow all trace of snow would be gone.

It was as we were stamping our boots, about to file in, that a resounding thud drew our attention. A young blackbird had collided with the window and lay, a tumbled heap of feathers, on the path. I darted to his rescue, but it was too late! He fixed me meekly with his beady eye and lapsed, quivering, into stillness. I stretched out a finger and stroked his soft wings. He was as warm as my own flesh and blood, poor scrap, so deceived by the reflected universe. I couldn't take it in. I fell on my knees and moaned and rocked to and fro and refused to be comforted. How could I bear such passive obedience to order?

That night, I had a nightmare about the hole in the garden and how it could be made good before Simms found out. I awoke, sobbing, to the recollection of yesterday and that precocious silence about which I could never speak.

# Morning

*He who binds to himself a joy*
*Doth the wingèd life destroy.*
*He who kisses the joy as it flies,*
*Lives in eternity's sunrise.*

# Morning

He had often promised that he would take me to the land of his ancestors. "There's nowhere like Scotland!" he would say. And I, fondly amused, vowed I'd no ear for the skirl of the pipes and no taste for that caustic liquor they drank. A pagan race, I told him. A purse-clutching folk. All the same, I knew we would go. Jude's plans, once articulated, always came to pass. First it was the glimmer of a new idea. Then he would stretch out his hands and feel the future tentatively, as if it were braille. The images would begin to teem, to coalesce into a picture. Slowly the vision loomed into focus and before I knew it, overwhelmed us in reality. There was never enough time to savour and possess it.

For our honeymoon, he had taken me to Norway. He was anxious to show me the Land of the Midnight Sun. After the wedding celebrations, when the piped lace on the cake, worked with agonising patience, had disintegrated, I would have preferred to linger for a day or two in a more familiar landscape. I would have preferred the calmer shores of Suffolk to the North Sea. I could dip my toes gingerly in at the water's edge along the solitary waste between Southwold and Leiston-cum-Sizewell, barbed with the horny limbs of crustaceans out of joint with their shells and twice the size of those on many a coast. I would have liked to walk barefoot and free for a day or so, making shallow impressions that could easily be effaced by the tide. But he was eager to cross the water, said if we missed the boat we'd have to wait days and days, heaven knew how long it would be, and the honeymoon would be over before it had begun. So we spent our wedding night in my bunk, in a cabin, in a boat out at sea. I embarked in a wide-brimmed hat adorned with ribbon. "Your mother chose it," I confessed with an apologetic laugh. "She said I ought to wear one. It's the done thing." "It is now," he joked and whipped it off and tossed it over the rail, leaving me suspended between laughter and tears. I watched it billow and float, billow and float, receding towards the misted harbour of Newcastle. When I met his eyes then, I knew it was for real, not a dream effervescing into nightmare. Intensely pleased with himself, he gave me a fulsome kiss, there and then on the deck in front of everyone. Folk exchanged glances, smiled indulgently. Our new clothes and the pastel confetti fluttering out of our shoes gave us away. Middle-aged women searched my face for signs of preparedness, recalling grim nights of betrayal. In their day, nice girls definitely *didn't* before the ring. I could see them thinking 'poor girl, on voyage, too,' when the mere fact of being at sea could so easily overset one's calm.

We stayed out for a long while, watching the ploughed foam disperse and marble the lucent green water. It grew dark. The boat begin to dip and rise.

But later, in the confines of the bunk, it was easier to forget you were all at sea with the sun gone down and the blinds drawn over the porthole. If the context was slightly dramatic, it seemed fitting, conducive to success. Intertwined beneath a blanket embossed with seagulls in flight, we discovered that we were after all in love. In the night, in the middle of the crossing where the water was deepest and the swell exaggerated the motion of the vessel, I realised with a burning twinge of that legendary pain, that I was not alone. I began to bubble softly with laughter at the facility with which my secretive body adapted to new rhythms. Touch and go, ebb and flow. Capering, scarpering. Deepening, sweeping up to a crest; acquiescence, quiescence. Sleep, drowned in a tide of radiant blood; lulled, both, by the ceaseless vibration.

In the morning, I peeped through the porthole and reported that there was still no land to be seen.

"It'll be within sight any time now," Jude promised, pulling a sweater over his eyes. And I believed him.

"This is the life!" he enthused, out on the deck after breakfast with spume flying into our faces. "Let's walk up to the sharp end, shall we? I'd rather see where we're going than where we've been!"

The floor pressed up under the soles of our feet. Jude took long strides, it didn't bother him.

"Look!" he cried, when I joined him at the rail. "There's land!"

Faint shadows loomed through an opal mist. "Isn't it a bank of cloud?"

"No, no," he said. "Terra firma. The outlines are too clear."

Gradually a long bare headland slid into view. It looked untamed, remote, belonging to nowhere. It was hard to imagine a whole country beyond. As the boat slipped into its lee, the wind dropped and the waves subsided. Soon another limb of land reached out on the other side. The course was scarcely ruffled now. Were it not for barren rocks jutting out of the water, we would have made rapid progress. Slowly we penetrated towards a harbour we could not see, expecting it to be around the next point, then the next. It was this anticipation that kept us standing there for nearly two hours. (The boat had glided so swiftly out of the dock at Newcastle.) We shuddered and put up our collars. The wind was less fierce, but the cold had built up under our clothes. Crowds gathered on deck.

At first there was little to see but the crude extremities hewn by a primeval hand and licked smooth as a bald pate by the sea in places. No beards of seaweed thrived in the ice-sharp air. Further on, brownish tufts of grass sprang out of the crevices; lichens mottled the rocks. I'd imagined it would be greener, but Jude said that wasn't until you were inland a bit, where the agriculture was. On the coast and up in the mountains it was pretty bleak. The time to see it was in the winter, when it was covered in snow!

Jude had been there before, not to discover the land and its inhabitants, nor even to see the Midnight Sun since it was the wrong time of year, but to ski. He had skimmed and swerved over the glistening surfaces. Everywhere looked like a Christmas cake then, the conifers feather-stitched against the sky. On the fourth day he had his leg in plaster and had to warm himself up with brandy for the rest of his stay.

We began to encroach upon the interior, picking our way through treacherous channels. We saw two or three summer dwellings made of timber, fragile as dolls' houses, perched in the nooks and crannies of the rockface. They were painted saffron, rust-red and green, all the colours flowing in the rock, so that they blended perfectly with the background. But despite the solid foundation, they looked tenuous, for all the world as if they might topple into the black lacquered water below.

Soon we caught sight of wharves, cargo boats, trawlers heaped with 'silver darlings', and then the outline of gabled roofs pinked against the dark slopes of the harbour. We smelled the saline smell of humanity torn between earth and water, and lost ourselves in the comings and goings on the borders of hope. Romantic Bergen, jewel of the Hanseatic League, overwhelmed us.

An hour later we were ashore, with the homeland of Ibsen rolling hard beneath our vehicle.

"The thing about Norway," I observed as we were driving through the orchard-clad slopes of Setesdal, "is that there's no sense of time, no history."

"No monuments, no crumbling ruins of the glorious past."

"There's nothing behind you. No evidence that anyone has been here before."

"They don't make their homes to last. They'd as lief chop down more timber and build new ones. In any case," Jude added, "the styles in architecture haven't altered much. At first glance, you can't really tell the old from the new."

I wondered if one needed to be an orphan or a gypsy, a wanderer severed from his heritage, in order to understand Norway; its raw, timeless mountains isolating one region from another. I knew, for Jude had told me, all about Norwegian mythology. How the forests and caves were riddled with trolls. One tree sprouting from their noses meant they were a hundred years old. Two trees, two hundred years. And when I saw giant profiles chiselled in the sullen granite by wind and weather, I realised how it had all evolved. So that was how they charted progress in this part of the world, by the changing face of the landscape itself rather than by any human achievement. This was the birthplace of *Peer Gynt* after all.

Even in that first week of marriage, I wished there were some way of conveying this to Jude. But he had his own way of looking at life.

"And another thing," he said, "there's no sense of distance, either. You look at a signpost and it dawns on you that the next place, all spelt out in capitals, is about ninety kilometres away. When you get there, it's just a hamlet with a shop and a petrol pump."

I couldn't help chuckling at his vexation. "It's all you need, isn't it?"

"All that travelling and getting nowhere!"

"They say it's the journey that counts."

The road in from the coast meandered through country as green as he'd promised, though with being so long under snow, it was only just regaining its verdure. The mad catharsis of spring had exposed matted, lacklustre turf, the fleshless bone of a harrowed land. Now its pile was lifting. The low slopes were laced with espaliered fruit trees, foaming with blossom and auguries of summer. Soft air had thinned the ice on the fiord, releasing waves suspended in flight by the sudden onset of biting weather. So abrupt, so insidious were the designs of winter, but as plain as watermarks in paper held up to the light.

Not even a breeze crêped the fluid surfaces. It was hard to tell the glassy world from the real one. But for that fine line of convergence, where reason intervened, it might have been impossible.

Later, several days later, we left the lower passes which ran like canyons between sheer sides of rock, cutting out the light and the views. The mountains seemed to hoard up their defences against the traveller. At this stage of the journey, they were as barriers rather than a means of protection. Even I was losing all inclination to linger. With gasps of satisfaction we greeted the broadening sky.

"You could travel on the main roads and get there faster," I said, "but you'd miss all this fantastic scenery."

"It's all right in the summer," Jude said, drawing up on a bend to make way for another car, "but it's a different kettle of fish in the winter. And that's most of the year. When the passes are blocked with snow, they won't clear them until they've enough motorists to make it worthwhile. You could be days late for an appointment. *Weeks!*"

I was amused by his injured faith. "But then, in the summer, they start resurfacing the roads."

"It's a fact. Life's tough in a land with few diversions."

Jude remarked how one mountain range gave upon another, how the layers of peaks accrued so that you never could see the light of perpetual day. Goats brooded over the sparse terrain, thriving apparently on nothing in particular. Their jangling movements underlined the loneliness, lent a haunting melody by the voracious silence. But for the occasional wagtail, there was no other sign of life. Fewer posts confirmed the way. There was no route now but the elected one. Just a chance reminder in case you had forgotten your destination, in case you had lost sight of your goal. The very road seemed less sure of itself, its surface badly fractured in parts. It crept furtively over narrow inclines, around sharp bends, cutting a gorge in deep drifts of insulated snow where diamond winds had tooled rocklike striations; echoes of the substantial. The distance was wreathed in a smoky haze, evoking long dark days in cramped dwellings and the inscrutable winter of the soul.

"I wonder the natives don't all emigrate," Jude said. "I wouldn't care to live here all the year round."

"They're happy enough, I expect. When you have to pit your wits against the objective, you don't *make* problems. All those new motorways at home peter out into complex traffic systems. It's still just as difficult to get where you want to be."

"What's the remedy, then? A standstill? No progress?"

"You have to work that one out for yourself."

We fell to laughter at the contentious mood which had overtaken us. We had seen enough for one day. We longed for nightfall that would shroud the mist-hung mountains and their weird vegetable mythology. We dined by candlelight and danced on polished pine floors in the bronze glow cast by an open log fire. We lost awareness of the darkling country outside as we slipped into a twilight euphoria misted with wine. Familiar tunes and rhythms, sounds not indigenous to this place, soothed our jagged nerves and we created a kind of harmony, the dream we had cherished on the far-of shores of home.

Afterwards, at the apex of our union, when the world spanned no more than the breadth of each other's arms, we would seem to *possess*. But the next morning, the spell was broken. Jude would be off again, dragging me from my cocoon, from sleep, physically, by hands and feet. "Come on," he'd coax, "there's so much to see! There's so much I want to show you!"

He showed me fresh peaks and ravines, inclines once buried under snow where he had skied. "Just look at that! I never knew there was a lake at the bottom! Ignorance is bliss!"

The innocent lake lapped idly against its shores and sent quivers along the bog-cotton reeds. It was clear, so clear in the shallows, as clear and soft as crystal. Wings of sunlight flashed over it with mesmerising constancy, too mercurial to admit the mirrored image. But the banks shelved steeply into waterworn boulders which gave way in turn to a fathomless abyss. Jude laughed in mock alarm. "Imagine it! Dicing with fate like that!" Though, in fact, it was possible to drive a vehicle over the frozen Norwegian waters in winter.

We travelled roads cleaving thick forests, fringed with rose bay willow herb echoing the shape of the conifers, where animals could flee from the hunter and the encroachments of civilisation. The only homesteads we came across were roofed with turf and barely distinguishable from the land itself, contained in an isolation so close to the beaten track. In the background, glaciers coruscated in the sun: near at hand, copper-green waterfalls crashed down from great heights, flinging out tiers of spray tinged with rainbows. Jude told me one was called The Bridal Veil. It was said that a French honeymoon couple had approached the bend above it too fast and had gone careering over the precipice.

A shadow fell over the sunny morning; a dark premonition of what I could not have explained. The hollow roar of the water conjured up the mournful but consonant baying of wolves. Poor couple, so recklessly happy as they plunged headlong to their doom. "It won't happen to us, will it?"

Jude laughed at my childlike terror and said he could think of worse ways to go. It must be awful to lose the use of one's faculties, one's awareness of life, as his father, a ponderous man, had done at the end. No, thank you, he said. "Anyway, it's too lovely a day to be moribund."

But I had glimpsed another side of the coin. Hadn't we seen how suddenly the climate could change across the summit's scythe edge? How the graphic landscape could pass into mist and grotesque distortion so that even the clouds lost their shape and form and there was only a negative print of the world?

It was a land of impossible concepts, Norway. A land of illusions, of boats suspended on liquid air. I came to think of our sojourn there as a blueprint for our life together.

Our first excursion to the Scottish Highlands had been in the nature of a holiday. For me, a time of enchanted discovery. For Jude, a time of expanded vision and possibilities explored. He saw the kingdoms of the world spread out before him. Soon he began to speak of developments areas, government grants, new horizons.

"It's like this, Angel," he said at supper one evening, playing chess with the pepper and salt mills. Pawn to King Four. "As I see it, the death sentence has already been passed. Our premises are too cramped for our rate of growth."

"You mean you'd move the business, lock, stock and barrel? Just uproot? Can you do that kind of thing?"

"Of course!"

"But what about your employees? You couldn't dismiss them all, could you?"

"Why not?"

I was speechless. The question hung between us. If Jude liked to get his own way, I had never believed him ruthless.

"That's the whole idea of these incentive schemes," he explained. "To recruit new labour where there's little industry. Where there's *space*."

"But many have given the firm years of loyalty."

"For crying out loud, we're not a charity! At least here in the Midlands there's a fair chance of other jobs. And they can come with us, those who want adventure."

"But how can they break with all they've known, just like that? Their lives are centred here, their history."

"They're born in a place and their content to die in it," Jude said dully.

"And you're not?"

"No, I'm bloody well not! We need wider scope, fresh ideas. Now's the time to move on. We can't *afford* to stand still."

Jude spooned dollops of mustard on to his plate and attacked his steak with customary zest. The pent-up tension seethed within him. You had the impression of someone trying to get away, a sprinter under starter's orders. Not for him my inner voyages as a struggling artist. The answer he strained for was always objective, always ahead, but advancing towards him through the cool blue tones of the middle distance. The gleam in his dark eyes was a gleam of resolution, not an absorbent gleam of understanding. In his genealogy, there was Jewish blood which no doubt accounted for his nomadic streak. "A cocktail of Jewish and Scots," I'd chaff him. "Heavens, Jude, you've got it made!"

"They have to suffer, the Jews," he said. "They're successful, but they have to suffer. They have to come to terms with exile."

I was surprised when he said this. I wondered why he had latched on to the fact.

"They're ever hopeful, that's for sure. Don't they have a saying, '*Next year in Jerusalem*'?"

Jude's grandfather, Benjamin Brightman, had founded the wallpaper business, now known as Harmony Wallcoverings, in the days of William Morris when flouncy petticoats were beginning to agitate beneath straitlaced bodices. In the company's annals, there were photographs fading to a sepia oblivion. He had been a liberal-minded gentleman with an interest in the Fabian movement, bearded, benign, a patriarch who won the affection of his employees by virtue of his social conscience.

Angus Brightman was less democratic in outlook. Though he showed a prudent benevolence towards the workforce and was not unconcerned about their personal problems, he ruled the business with a rod of iron. He refused to delegate and instituted a 'no risks' policy which drove Jude insane when he joined the firm and later became a director. The ensuing conflict was not merely of youth versus age, but of gambler versus miser. The business was the butt of two opposing philosophies and each more deeply confirmed the other in his beliefs.

Since Angus' death, some months after Jude and I were married, the business had burgeoned. Jude had given full rein to his plans. He chanced his arm and trebled the turnover in no time at all. He was, he discovered, blessed with the Midas Touch; a genius for acting on the spur of a propitious moment. No one was going to thwart him now!

"Something's happened to you," he said with a hint of accusation. "You thought the Highlands idyllic when we went last year."

"I can't paint," I moaned. "My head is a turmoil of lucid thoughts, displaced, welling up from nowhere. They won't make a picture."

"What you need is a change of scene. New horizons."

"It won't make me forget the baby..." We had conceived our stillborn child, a son, in Scotland.

"Your creative impulses have been stifled. Mine have, too. We need a *break*."

I shrank from the notion. My whole being protested. Inside three years of marriage, our slate cottage in the Charnwood Forest was already our second home. My eye skimmed over the furniture we'd shared such delight in choosing, and the artefacts brought back from our trips abroad; the hearthrug from Marrakesh, the frilly glass trumpets that were lampshades from Murano; the shell from the Indian Ocean, a transcendent shade of aquamarine lined with pearl and grained with feathery waves; the burnished steel cutlery from Kristiansand; the tapestry from Rome, the Klimt mosaic from Vienna. Would these objects re-assemble elsewhere and blend into a new scheme? And would that place be Home?

"I do worry about you, Jude, always giving up the present for the sake of the future, never happy for long in one place."

"I see no virtue in getting into a rut. We're not gypsies. We won't be moving on for ever. Once we get there, we'll settle down."

There were days when I thought *Why me?* and my palate was tainted with bitterness. And there were days when I knew that all things were ordained and a curious sense of safety surrounded me. I was enclosed within a bubble that nothing could prick.

The shining days fell unannounced between the days of dark despair, lying like golden coins at the bottom of a well. It was then that I truly believed I would recover. But on the bad days I saw that nothing altered the pattern of elation and despair. I brimmed with anxiety and was convinced that Jude ought to know. He might be burdened by remorse later if he didn't. I'd read a magazine feature about terminal illness which spoke of the wisdom of honesty. Relationships had time to mend, or to become stronger against the parting, a truer set of values was forged so that when the sick person passed on, the gap would close, the flesh would heal and the scars would not be scored too deeply. The trauma, if not the grief, was forestalled.

All the same, some instinct within me fought shy of the ordeal. I kept putting off the evil moment because, nowadays, it is easier to bypass death than to cast about for a means of approach. It is easier to regret things said than unsaid. And, of course, there *could* be a miracle. I might go to Lourdes in a Jumbulance – that would be travelling to some purpose! – or a pilgrimage to Medjugorge or Assisi. *I could.* Plus, there was constant medical research going on and always the chance of a tremendous breakthrough.

As one day passed into the next and life followed its formulaic pattern, it was easy to believe this. So what good was there to be gained from telling Jude? I couldn't bear to see him chafing at the bit, keeping a vigilant eye on the slightest relapse, waiting for me to die. Life must go on, risks must be taken. He had his future to make and I ought not to prejudice his judgment. I would strive to bury my personal feelings and be as happy as possible so that he had no cause to reproach himself later. He must carry out his plans since the time seemed ripe. Those who suffered bereavement said that a quantity of work and the sheer force of routine carried one through the first desolate months. Our removal to Scotland was a God-given gift. I remembered how he'd once transplanted a laurel in the middle of June because he was remodelling the garden and didn't have the patience to let another year lapse. He'd smiled at my caution, my frowns, as I watched him dig. "What's up? I'm blessed with the golden touch, aren't I?" I had to agree that it was so. Even the laurel had flourished, though its fate hung in the balance for several months.

I had known my fate since the last day of December when ice was set taut over the garden pond and the trees glittered with rime. The land lay undisclosed behind thick fog. Only the dark cracks of skeletal trees showed here and there. That night we were going to a party. Jude felt it would do me good.

When I knocked on the surgery door and entered, knowing the limited time for such consultations, I automatically expected to find Dr. Wells absorbed in an overflow of note-taking from the previous patient and was prepared for an air of offhand interest. Instead his gaze was fixed on the open file on his desk.

"Come in, Mrs Brightman. Sit down. How are you today?" he enquired with devious solicitude. His eyes swerved towards me and away again. The patient's chair was set, not opposite his, but at an angle to it, creating a line of vision with an expanded model of the inner ear. "I'm sorry, the central heating isn't working. I hope it wasn't too chilly in the waiting room."

I sensed a fissure in his mask. "No," I said. "I didn't notice." A fan heater was working in the consulting room.

"I have here the hospital's report..."

My sinews tensed. After the miscarriage, I was subjected to a series of tests and probes which included an electrocardiogram. Several specialists had been drawn into conference and seemed reluctant to discharge me from hospital. Just routine, Mrs Brightman, they assured me with bluff congeniality, leaving me to conclude that all was being done in the interest of future pregnancies. Unsettling as it was, I didn't suppose there was anything seriously wrong. If I was inclined to tire easily, I had learnt to adapt to my limitations and enjoyed good health on the whole.

"And...?"

"Mrs Brightman," he addressed me solemnly, "I'm afraid I have to tell you that you must not expect to have another child."

A baby's cry echoed along the corridor of the Health Centre and seemed to articulate some inner cry of my own. I had spoken to our unborn child, told him how much I loved him and how beautiful the world was, and not long after the 'quickening', he had responded with a gentle thrust. I know that it was so; I didn't imagine it. In a moment of utter anguish, I realised that it was the only dialogue I would ever have with someone of my own flesh and blood. I would never be in touch with my mysterious forebears through the rising generation.

I could not bear to think of the barren years ahead, nor the cradle in the nursery remaining empty. Our son had been born about ten weeks before term, just large enough to have survived with intensive care had there been a spark of life in him. They had whisked him away, not wishing to add to my distress. It wasn't fashionable to mourn. A cheery nurse had pointed out that as I was young and it was my first pregnancy, the usual advice was to conceive again with all possible haste. But that did not fill my aching arms for the unique individual I *was expecting*. I felt friendless and bruised to the core. In the end, I locked myself into a bathroom, which patients were strictly forbidden to do, and ran water to drown the sound of my weeping until, my absence noted, they came banging on the door, chiding me for my folly. "You might have fainted, Mrs Brightman! And then, what?"

The telephone on the desk gave a siren ring. Dr. Wells was urgently needed in another part of the building. He protested but finally excused himself, hastening from the room with an air of reprieve.

The heater whirred, wafting its sterile warmth towards me. Through a glass panel in the door, I could see a poster outlining the benefits to be claimed in pregnancy. I turned to the upside down report with its short chronicle of trial and failure, indelible script filling the spaces between blocks of print. A several-digit number was scribbled in pencil at the top. The shape of it alerted me. It was the number I dialled for Jude's office. With deft facility, I slid the file round, it was over in a second. Advanced Mitral Stenosis, I read. Those three words leapt out at me from the wiry jumble of notes, rebounding senselessly in my brain. I chased scraps of information gleaned from the radio, from a piece I had once read in the *Nursing Times* which some fateful premonition must have caused me to heed. I was counting the windowpanes now, assessing the width and depth of them. A ladybird, confused by the interior climate, was groping up the glass, slipping, striving again. It landed on the frame. Mitral Stenosis. A narrowing of valves, a closure of the ways. There was no recommendation for surgery.

I trembled at what I had done. I was in possession of knowledge I was never meant to have. I felt like a culprit on the wrong side of the law, sitting there as immobile as stone.

And then, as the hiatus opened, it seemed that life had been lived for this. All I had gone through had been a preparation for death.

When Dr. Wells returned, he glanced at me covertly, seeing the disturbed papers I'd made no attempt to replace. For it could not be righted, knowledge of death. It could not be put in its place.

"How long?" I asked tonelessly, focused on space. "How long is there left?"

"You have youth on your side..."

"Please..."

"A year. Maybe more. My dear, I...I'm terribly sorry."

"Can...nothing be done, nothing at all? I thought..."

"In some instances, surgery is feasible. In your case, there are complications."

His traitor's eye met mine. "Thank you," I said. "Thank you for telling me."

One year. Two. I thought of all the living that had to be compacted into that year, the places I must see, the pictures I must paint. Already my being had catapulted itself into the future and I wanted desperately to be out there. Outside. Beginning it all. The image of Jude stabbed me with pain. I thought of the way be preferred his omelettes and who would iron his shirts. My throat was dry as tinder. It ached and ached like limbs submerged in iced water.

"My husband doesn't...know?"

"Not yet. I would appreciate a talk with him."

"No!" I managed to curb my alarm. I could feel my personhood slipping away. Everything decided over my head. My opinion, at best, indulged. "I'd rather handle it myself. At least let me do that."

He considered this doubtfully, but then nodded. It was plain he did not want the duty anyway. "All right. If that's what you wish."

His pen began to glide over the prescription pad. "I'll put you in contact with a palliative care nurse. If there's any way at all *we* can help, please don't hesitate to ask. Live as you think best. You will probably experience periods of strain and fatigue and periods of remission. These should help when you're going through a bad patch. And these," he explained, adding a second line, "should be taken all the time. I'll arrange for repeat prescriptions to be left at Reception for you." He tore off the leaf and handed it over. "I'll ask Sister to give you something now, and then to run you home if she's free."

"Thank you, but there's no need. Really there isn't. Please don't trouble."

He sat with the receiver poised in mid-air. Dead leaves captured by a breath of wind swirled over the forecourt. I noticed that his car was parked exactly between the white lines in his allotted space. He replaced the receiver.

As I made to leave, he got up and mechanically washed his hands at the sink.


But outside and alone, I didn't know whether to turn to left or to right. I wanted human contact, the sound of an ordinary voice and the reassuring surface of things. My feet began to conduct me along the pavement, bereft of sensation, and the clamorous world passed me by.

At length, I realised that I was going the way I had come. I was treading a path to somewhere I knew. I was going home. There were ashes sprinkled on the ground where the overflow leaked.

I slid the key into the lock and opened the door. The faded smell of lasagne and stale pot-pourri greeted me. Now I could rest. I was released of the effort of having to get by. The emptiness was astounding. And the crushing truth was borne in upon me that it wasn't here that I wanted to be, for this place was full of the mementoes of the life I must leave. In a daze I went from room to room, seeing the house through a new pair of eyes. Already it had assumed an independent identity. It was impressed with my stamp and yet not *mine*.

On the spur of the moment, I ran out of the door and down the path into the wood, the side gate whining on its rusty hinges. I had to escape but did not know where to go. The pear tree by the hedge was a ravelled confusion of branches. The winter trees, choked in the stranglehold of ivy, loomed large on all sides. I hurried on through the chill mist until the pain in my chest reached explosion pitch and I stumbled and fell. My boots were not walking boots, not fitted for uncertain terrain. My hands shot out and groped among the withered leaves coated with pinpoints of frost. My fingers, closing upon them, burnt cold. Leprous colonies of fungi stained the soured earth, redolent of decay. The world tilted and righted, tilted and began to spin, forcing me down against the hardened ground. My mind could gain no foothold and, even shutting out the day, I could not focus on the darkness within. All my strength was sapped by the sheer effort of existing. "Oh God," I cried in a whisper, "help me!"

A calm began to descend. My breath had melted a clear patch in the frost. There were winged seeds among the relics of summer. Keys. I brushed them from my coat and, to my surprise, saw that the drifting fog was stealing away so that a mossy track unfurled in a long vista between the trees and brambles. A dry-stone wall bounded the wood and beyond it the reservoir was coming into view, rimmed with ice and bullioned by perch rising for air. The words came to me: *Cast your net on the right side.* The bright side. The positive side. What other way was there to cross the void yawning at my feet? Those fishermen, long ago in Galilee, toiling all night to the point of exhaustion, had been so near yet so far from a yield.

I turned back to the cottage, a heavy languor weighing upon my limbs, and kicked off my boots and sank on to the bed and slept soundly for four or five hours.

That evening, when the beam of Jude's headlights turned full upon the house, I was ready to meet him.

"What did the Doc say?" he asked, taking the newspaper from his brief-case. The locks snapped shut. His beloved, too human face turned towards me, so charged with life and exchanges from the outside world. My courage failed.

"Oh, my circulation's not as good as it might be," I told him, astonished at my facility for prevarication. The role was thrust upon me unrehearsed and was the more eloquent for it. "He's given me some pills."

"What you need is lots of fresh air. Didn't I tell you that?"

"I must change for the party. We don't want to be late," I said, thinking that *Auld Lang Syne* might prove too much.


"Of course," Jude admitted, "there are a lot of bridges to cross before we can make a move."

Stacey's cat from the nursery over the way, risked the breach between the side wall and the fence where it could keep a close eye on the comings and goings in the nest box. Its claws achieved a precarious purchase on the post, its tail moving rhythmically to and fro.

"I wish I could rely on the full support of the Board."

"Can't you?"

"Neil Porteous is all for the idea. Jack Vincent's undecided. Adrian Stokes is against. Well, that's to be expected, he's coasting to retirement. Set in his ways is Adrian. But it's Mother I can't fathom. She's got a bee in her bonnet about something."

"You may need her casting vote."

"You reckon? Time for a chinwag over lunch on Sunday. Then we can convene a meeting. There are some premises up in Tayside, on an industrial estate, that would suit us down to the ground."

Fleetingly, I experienced a strange sensation of detachment. He was shrinking away from me. He seemed to be speaking 'out there' in another dimension of irrelevant things. "You'll have to rent, won't you?" I heard myself say. "You can't run to buying."

"Whatever we do, we've got to move fast. Our whole future's at stake!"

But it was not of the future I wanted to think. My life belonged to the past. Scenes from earlier days came up vividly before me. Days lost and irretrievable, days within the compass of my own history spun out of dimmer days stretching back into the far reaches of Time.

Oh, he had taken me on so many diverting journeys! Not only the Land of the Midnight Sun had he wanted to show me, but ancient civilisations and oases fanned by palms. He would like, he announced in a moment of pure exhilaration, for us to make love in every capital in the world. He would show me the Seven Wonders and the places of pilgrimage. We were conquerors of Time and Space, traversing oceans and deserts in the twinkling of an eye, jetting towards some target on the fragmented plates of the globe. We'd seen cities astride fault lines, defying the cataclysm. And temples upon outcrops of rock above seas of clear turquoise, bays flooded with carmine as daylight faded. We'd explored the labyrinths of Crete and were overawed by the apocalyptic domes of Venice; way behind us, the sleepy spires of home. Yes, there were many such visions, all tarnished and corroded at close range from the miasmas of progress. Jude was always anxious to move on, be elsewhere.

Most haunting of all was the spirit of Greece. Athens, wreathed in a purple mote haze on a brilliant morning, dominated still by its archaic culture. Even after centuries and two thousand years of Grace, you could forget, on such a day, that any change had taken place.

I recalled the tunnel-like echo of its streets, the vehicles that tore and screamed around the Squares; the plangent music issuing from every *taverna*, drowning the welter of passions and sorrows within; the subdued old men, work-hewn and weary, bewitched by the anodyne glint of *retsina* and *ouzo*; the riots before dawn and the suffocating illusions of liberty; the emollient odour of olives that clung to the clothes and the Turkish coffee silting the cup. And at every street corner, at every entrance and exit, the lottery tickets...

We had travelled to Corinth, I remembered it well. The road followed the craggy littoral of the Saronic Gulf, then veered into Peloponnesus, over the Corinth Canal, narrow and straight as a die. We had peered in wonder down the sheer-sided passage at the ribbon of water below, so deep that huge vessels looked lost in the chasm and the bridge lodging across the top, so frail.

Like a camera with an angle on its own particular story, my mind enlisted other scenes. Ancient Corinth abandoned by the receding tide, out of joint with the modern port. Part of it had been excavated and the lineaments traced of what was still buried. Here and there posts marked the depths of previous digs. They had plans, the archaeologists, the Departments of Classical Studies, they knew in some detail what was secreted beneath the shuttered villas and the groves of orange and lemon.

But clearest of all was the memory of Jude motionless! He was standing where St. Paul was reputed to have preached to those hedonistic Corinthians, grown complacent in prosperity, lured into the path of courtesans whose shoes printed the words 'follow me' in the sand. His imagination was fired as he gazed out towards the bay, seeing ships laden with cargo, bound for the ends of the earth. An endless traffic of coveted wares and an economy wrought with undisciplined gifts. When his thoughts snapped back to the present, he said: "What's so staggering about all this is that it's taken so long to discover. It's been here all the time, forgotten for centuries, and no one's bothered until now to find it. Why is that?"

I was amused at the time by his preoccupation with this question. It had seemed so important to him. Two years later, I had the answer. A chilling answer. I knew because of what was happening to me. It was because the world itself was dying that it had taken to delving into the past, as the old do, and those upon whom the future has shut down, investing memories with a life the reality has often failed to own. The discoveries made in the fields of archaeology and psychology, the nostalgia for things past, revisionist history and the speculation on the origins of mankind and his universe, all seemed to betoken a creation in its latter stages; a creation without a tomorrow. After two World Wars and the intensifying threat of a nuclear holocaust, there was not much left for people to believe in. A void loomed ahead which they saw no means of spanning. So the world closed its door upon the inevitable, sealed up the cracks against death and destruction, and got on with the business of its technological advances which some claimed would deliver it.

Here my despair reached saturation point. The world had no future and neither had I. What was the purpose of existence at all? What was it but a god-awful joke practised for the amusement of a Divine Power? I wept because I had lost my baby and I couldn't paint. All I could do was to jot down scattered thoughts on torn-off scraps of paper, leave them to get lost among the outstanding bills.

*I can't go on.*

But I already had! That day I was forced to face the truth at the Health Centre, I had begun a different journey. A path opened up in the woods. *Cast your net on the right side.* The only thing to do was to create an alibi for existing, to build a bridge between the known and the unknown and drive oneself across it, refusing to look down at the bottomless gulf below. *That* was life!

"Of course," Jude had said, "there are a lot of bridges to cross before we can make a move!"


Jude knew that something was afoot the day his mother appeared in peacock blue. He was even more astonished when he caught the flash of scarlet and regal purple among the sugared almond pastels thronging the rail of her wardrobe

"She's getting out of hand," he reported. "I don't know what's got into her."

Hitherto, my mother-in-law, Eudora, had been quite a tractable sort, a fortunate thing for Jude since she was the Company Chairman and had the casting vote on any issue on which the Board was divided. Once or twice a week he would so far subscribe to filial duty as to drop in for sherry on his way home from the office. She liked to be kept informed of events and this was a good time to insinuate some of his more controversial ideas, thus preparing the ground for the next meeting when the matter would be debated in earnest. Eudora idolised Jude and could always be relied upon to see his point of view. Her outlook was largely mounted upon borrowed opinions and Jude felt he would be a fool not to cash in. Besides, she'd no complaints: swelling dividends had been the consolation of her widowhood.

But around the time his mother's wardrobe began to resemble the visual spectrum, Jude had an idea his ascendancy was being challenged. Eudora developed a habit of arguing, just for the sake of it. When he alluded, not for the first time, to the need to seek more capacious premises, she countered him with phrases about 'overstretching oneself'. Was it wise, she asked, to take risks in the present climate? Wouldn't it be better to *consolidate*, darling?

The extraneous word 'consolidate' made his defences bristle. It reminded him of his father. But he knew that for her, Angus' ghost had long been laid. It had receded to a safe distance and two dimensions upon the boardroom wall where it cast a keen eye over the proceedings and caused some to shudder at the recollection of his booming voice. Now the tenor of her life had changed. She was no longer in the shadow of an awe-inspiring despot; she had come to interpret the world in her own pallid colours. Nor was she one of nature's 'consolidators' herself. She could justify any extravagance with the 'charity begins at home' maxim.

No, Jude fancied he could scent some other influence. Some other light was reflected in the shallow convex of her eye. "Don't tell me" he probed, "you're losing confidence in the management. You can take it from me we're an extremely healthy concern, on the up and up. What we do have to borrow will be paid off in a year or two with increased production and sales."

Eudora said in a charming, evasive way: "Well, darling, one does glance at the City Page from time to time and it's so frightfully gloomy isn't it? Full of Bulls and Bears!"

He'd never known her look at anything but the headlines and the cookery features. Not that the culinary arts appealed to her much, but she did enjoy collecting recipes to exchange over a cosy chat at the Bridge Club.

Finally, he decided that the best thing to do was to broach his plans over our Sunday meal while I was there to support him. When we skidded to a halt on the red tarmac of his mother's neo-Georgian house, the garage doors were wide open to reveal an old Rolls Royce Silver Dawn in pristine condition in the long empty space. "Looks as though she's got guests," Jude said.

Sometimes, he had the impression, when he crossed the threshold, that the iron had gone out of the superstructure since his father's demise. Those terse, resounding tones no longer made the rafters ring or chafed the delicate membranes of the mind! For it was a fact that the old man's habits of consolidation were ingrained. He could no more leave them at the office than his paunch or his mulish gait, but brought them even to the breakfast table. "Look at you, Mother," he would roar, "there's a month's ration of butter on that piece of toast!" "Yes, dear, it's a miracle we managed," she would meekly reply, spreading the clot of butter over the toast until it was thoroughly sodden and less incriminating and thinking that they never would have survived if it hadn't been for one or two of her little black market deals. For she was adept at the craft of self-preservation and managed to extract monthly cheques for housekeeping far in excess of requirements, siphoning off the handsome balance into her 'nest-egg' account. Fortunately, for all his bluff and bluster, Angus hadn't the first notion of domestic economy, though it had been his life's endeavour to simulate the conditions of wartime. Not only did it create the right climate for his belligerent nature, but gave full rein to a parsimonious streak. "No sense of values, that's the trouble with folk today!"

However, no such memory seemed to oppress Jude on that occasion. There was a vital air about the place, an air of precipitation. The hall with its dark oak panelling was brightly splashed with daffodils and tulips. The moment she heard the turn of the handle, Eudora Brightman came rushing out to meet us, wafting a heady scent. She was wearing a wine velvet suit with a spray of freesias clasped in a posy-holder on her shoulder.

"Mother, you look marvellous! Doesn't she, Angie?"

We greeted her with an exaggerated peck.

"Darlings," she whispered excitedly, linking arms with both of us in a conspiratorial fashion, "there's someone I'd like you to meet. He's rather special. My bridge partner, you know!"

Jude and I caught each other's eye in amusement as she frogmarched us into the drawing-room where a tall gentleman had installed himself with his backside to the open fire. He struck a military attitude with his feet apart and his hands linked behind his back in readiness to inspect the troops. There was a faintly patronising air about him of someone who has taken possession and is fully accustomed to holding the fort. He had bland, full features and a circumflex moustache thatching a rather petulant upper lip.

"Julius, my son and his wife. Meet Colonel Raven," sang Eudora, her freesias quivering.

After she had fussed over the introductions, she said she must see how the food was coming along, charging Jude to operate the decanter, darling, do. Be sure and give the Colonel the dry, he was sweet enough! Gunilla, her homesick Swedish maid, would probably be weeping over the sauce.

We sat down. Colonel Raven squinted through the golden lights of his glass. "Y'mother tells me you're thinking of branching out," he commented.

"Not branching out so much as transplanting ourselves," Jude revised, instinctively on the defensive.

"Indeed? You mean abandon base and set up camp elsewhere?"

"That's the general idea."

"Your chaps won't like that, will they?"

47

"We're prepared to help with the rehousing of those who want to join us. Those who don't will have to earn corn elsewhere. We're hoping to take key personnel with us."

"And where do you propose to do that?"

"Tayside," Jude said. "Or at any rate one of the development areas up in Scotland. We envisage recruiting extra labour."

"Risky business," the Colonel said with a dubious curve of his mouth. "Can't tell where things are heading. Strikes! All this damned Government intervention and no spending money about." Colonel Raven lived with his spinster daughter, the headmistress of a private girls' school. He tended to have acerbic views on politics.

Jude twizzled the stem of his glass so that the angle of light rotated. "We're looking to give our image a much higher profile. Have to be competitive nowadays or go under. We've had new machines on order for a twelvemonth and there's simply nowhere for them to go. We need height as well as breadth for our kind of plant."

If I felt an impulse to defend Jude, it was less because he was under attack than because I was struggling to efface my own doubts about the scheme. "And you can get grants to relocate in Scotland," I added.

Colonel Raven sniffed. "All the same, m'dear, it's not all a bed of roses getting away from the hub of things. At present you're well positioned for distribution. Helps to keep prices down. But it seems you've got y'campaign pretty pat. Obviously gone into it thoroughly."

"We have," Jude assured him. "We've seen this coming for a while. We've had to keep it under our hats, though. Didn't want our employees to get wind of it too early. Nor did we want our plans leaking to our rivals."

"Take the enemy unawares, what!"

At the table, nothing more was said about Scotland. The Colonel tucked his napkin under his chin and fell to with unbridled appetite. Avocadoes with smoked salmon. Pork *snitzel* with asparagus, wild mushrooms and Lyonnaise potatoes. A well-rounded Alsatian Riesling to stimulate the palate. And for dessert, French apple tart with Chantilly cream, all melting on the tongue. This was how they dined in the hall of the gods! Apparently, he was used to cold shoulder and stewed fruit at home, frugally irrigated with evaporated milk.

We finished eating and, before the Colonel could start reminiscing, as he was inclined to do during the process of digestion, Eudora bade us withdraw to the conservatory where we could relax amid her copious greenery over coffee and liqueur chocolates. When she had established that her special guest desired nothing further, she put her hand on his arm, saying, "Julius, you must take a peep at my garden. You've never seen it in daylight, have you, dear?"

He patted his satisfied belly, his eyes twinkling. "Decent spot of grub, what! Now for a patrol of the estate!"

"Whisper it low," Eudora confided as they went arm in arm out of the door, "but I think my yucca plant is going to flower this year. Such a rare event! We've had to move it, though. Brabbs tells me a sunny patch and well-drained soil are the best conditions. To think it's been in the shade all this time!"

I watched them through the window. Around the borders they went, treading over rust-edged blossom, dodging the lithe extensions of young branches, he clumsily, she with exaggerated care. The garden was striped with shadows plain as statements. The air was clear, too clear. A storm was brewing.

"Whew!" Jude whistled as though he had narrowly escaped a misfortune. He looked up from his Sunday crossword, frustrated by black squares in all the wrong places. "What do you make of that?"

"What should I make of it?"

"I don't like the way Mother's playing up to that fellow. It's not decent at their age."

"It could be a blessing. It might take the edge off losing you."

"He's an eye to the main chance, that's what!"

I chuckled at the idea of a genteel, if not wealthy, Colonel having designs on the modest fortune of a wallpaper widow. "He's the sort who's fond of his comforts, yes. But why shouldn't he make capital out of your mother's extravagance if it makes them both happy?"

Jude did not care for this image of united strength. "Whose side are you one, anyway?"

I glanced towards the lawns on the other side of the glass, and then at Jude among the exotic plumes of his mother's plants. I did not want to join battle, but there were some issues which could not be dodged. Jude said: "I wonder if the time has come to persuade her to stand down from the Chairmanship."

"In favour of whom? You?"

"Well, I can't see that there could be any *concrete* objection. It won't affect her income. She'll still reap a dividend from the Trust, Dad's shares that I'll be getting when she dies. Her own shares she intends to make over to me soon anyway. It helps to reduce estate duty, apparently. Prideaux, her accountant, was waffling on about it the other day."

It was obvious what Jude might hope to achieve by these manoeuvres. "She's unlikely to agree to that, wouldn't you say, with something against her interests in the offing?"

"Even so," Jude insisted, "our meetings will have to be handled properly once we get this venture off the ground. We'll be in the big league then."

I was weary. I wanted only to sit by the window, unmolested, and gaze. For what had his dreams, his ambitions, to do with me? There were moments when I thought I did not know him at all, when life eddied around me and receded, never claiming me for its own.

*Where had I come from and where was I going?*

But there, cast adrift, when I least expected an anchor, I saw that while the horizon faded, the foreground was shifting into a beautiful perspective. The distant past and the future were linked and lost in infinity and I was standing at the one shining point in the revolution, the present. Everything I looked upon was bathed in the same supernal gold, illumined from within. All things profoundly *were*.

I heard far off, as in a dream, distracted proclamations of an Energy Crisis. I knew it in flesh and bone! Sooner or later, almost every day now, there came a moment when vitality cut out. Strive as I might, I couldn't drive myself back into its flow. But how different this new order was! An essence of light and power suffused every nerve, never returning as a heartbeat does to its source for impetus. Colours glowed with a soft translucence. Grass greener than any on the other side seemed to suck me through the dark void of the eye into its virescence.

"A penny for them."

The flame was slowly quenched. The world froze into its harsh symbolic pose once more. Jude was watching me, his attention caught by my incommunicable repose. Yet for me, the defences were down. I was open to him. I knew who it was over there, he in his place, me in mine. But how to answer him, how to make some exchange, was beyond me. *"A penny for them."*

"The trouble is," Jude was saying, "I can't see my way clear."

"No."

Overhead the sky was lustreless as undipped fleece. The day lapsed into forgetting.

"I'm going out there. I'm going to tell her. No time like the present."

Then he was gone. He strode across the grass, the flattened blades springing erect in his wake. On the table, the crossword was left unfinished beneath his Parker ballpoint.

Looking out on the garden, I could see the three of them, Jude, his mother and the Colonel, grouped uncertainly about the spiky yucca. They moved like characters in a Russian play, with an air of passive discontent. The sun squinted down upon them brilliantly, then died. The formation broke. The shadows pulled apart so that the concentrated stain they made upon the earth was dispersed. The garden shivered. Trees let fall a shower of petals which were caught up everywhere in invisible webs.

"If you don't mind, this is a family affair," Jude rebuked the Colonel when we were all by the fire again.

"Jude!" shrieked his afflicted parent, "don't speak to him like that! *He is practically one of the family.*"

The guest was visibly unhappy at finding himself in the front line. Having received the offensive, he decided that a retreat was called for. Engagement on enemy territory was a distinct disadvantage.

"Got my marching orders so I'd best be off, Eudora. See you when I do."

"How can you be so unfeeling, Jude? That my own son should act in such an ill-bred manner. After all the years I've devoted to your upbringing. And to think your poor father sold the Sargent in order to send you to public school!" The deluge began in earnest. Eudora fished up her sleeve and produced a flimsy handkerchief. "Oh, the life of it I had with him!"

For the first time in decades, Eudora had surprised real life unfolding before her, new possibilities were prising the way open. She saw herself *established*, the dashing widow and figurehead of an empire. The young folk would be in regular attendance at her court. They would bring their children to tea on Sunday. She would be forever on call, meeting frantic appeals for a babysitter with regal generosity. And, of course, there would be her new consort, Julius, stepping into Angus' shoes. The elegant fortress she had raised against death and despair was crumbling before her eyes. The awful truth was dawning. Life was not going to be her guest tomorrow, or the next day, or on some nebulous day to come. The long years of waiting and preparation, of watching untenable structures collapse, were for nothing. *This was it.*

"I might just as well have brought out the Waterford crystal, my Dresden and diamonds, all the linen and blankets and Jubilee bells saved from the January sales," she reflected mournfully, "for no one will want them."

Deep down, she had never forgiven me for losing the baby. It was linked in her mind with disaster. The whole business of Jude's marriage had been eminently tiresome, though necessary for the procreation of grandchildren and all the compensations they would bring. I was not the daughter-in-law she would have chosen, however, with my unfortunate background and focused mind. And she was in no way a surrogate mother to me. I had a mother who had balked at motherhood while the Blessed Virgin alone held out her arms to me.

"You simply can't change your ways at my time of life, move, start a new network. What would become of Julius?" she sobbed. "I've lived in this house since your father brought me back from India when I was a gel without the slightest notion of how to cook or *scrimp* or mend a seam!"

I put a comforting arm around her. "We shall visit you sometimes. And you can come and stay with us whenever you wish."

"It isn't the same, all that distance away. You don't understand," wept Eudora, and the hurt revived all the other hurts she had ever received. "You don't understand. *It's all right for you. You've got youth and life on your side.*"

Hail spattered the windowpanes like grapeshot. A cinder fell into the hearth, smouldered and extinguished itself.

"If it's any consolation," I said quietly, "I don't want to go either. But there's a right time for everything. A season."

Fired, Jude began to enlarge upon his plans. He was not ineloquent as he sat astride a spoonback chair, gripping its frame, and sketched for us a dramatic picture which featured soaring rates of inflation and slumps in the market. His mother revived somewhat when she heard the term 'injection of capital'. Harmony could buy bigger, make faster, which would offset the increased cost of human resources and raw materials. It was imperative that we keep abreast of international competition. "We're aiming to launch a whole new range of designs," Jude announced triumphantly. "Our Cosmos Collection."

Eudora averted her face and contemplated forbidding skies.


"It could be difficult without her vote," I said on the way home. I wondered if it was an omen, if fate were intervening on my behalf to check Jude. We had come to a gated road and he was first out of the car to fling it wide, pulling on the handbrake with one hand, opening the door with the other.

"Difficult," he agreed, accelerating with a skid. "Difficult, but not impossible. Nothing's that."

A week later, Jude flew to Scotland and returned armed with fresh evidence to strengthen his case. That morning he took his leave early with a quick kiss at the door. "I'm off then," he'd said. "Off to pan for gold!" He was poised for flight. There was a glint in his eye and I knew that what was in prospect would soon be upon us. He was never daunted for long.

Sure enough, he returned bursting with tales of promise. The land of his ancestors was indeed a land of abundance. He turned up his brief-case over the coffee table and sheaves of literature slithered out. He pointed to this, emphasised that, drew little diagrams with such deft strokes of his pen. He'd taken a quick look at several sites, but the Tayside development was ideal for his purpose. He'd found exactly the right premises, just waiting to be occupied. He'd seen a house, too, a Victorian villa built of glistening granite with four bedrooms and any number of outhouses, in two acres of ground. "Beautiful sloping lawns," he said with a sweeping gesture, "all covered with daffodils. I'll take you as soon as the meeting's over. You'll love it."

An atmosphere of tense exhilaration reigned in the Boardroom when I arrived at five to eleven to hear the debate. Eudora Brightman turned up, dead on time, in black and white buttoned up to the chin. Her cheeks were pinched with spots of colour, her eyes bright as a robin's.

"Let it be known," she announced when the minutes had been read and the business declared, irrespective of her role as Chairman, "that I am totally against this proposal. Inflation calls for retrenchment, not uninhibited spending!"

Light dilated on the wall in the area of Angus' portrait. It was odd that Eudora should find herself cramped by her own style and have to resort to the expedient of his. How he would have cheered! I knew the light had caught Jude's eye, too. It spurred him on, kept the adrenalin flowing. He cleared his throat apologetically on behalf of his parent and re-aligned the papers in his folder.

"Thank you, Mother. We shall be recording our votes in due course. Meanwhile you may be persuaded to change your mind, as ladies are not unknown to do on occasion, when we have discussed the findings of my recent visit to Perth. You have all received a copy of my report."

In the event, Jude could afford to be confident, as his mother soon realised, however intransigent her position. Much to her chagrin, the others were unanimously in favour. Not only had the pro-expansionists gained the wavering allegiance of Jack Vincent, but apologies for absence were received from Adrian Stokes. He wished to abstain from voting since his closeness to retirement might be deemed to prejudice the issue. It was decided to retire him early with a golden handshake and moved that John Meredith, the firm's talented young accountant, who espoused the cause, be invited to join the Board. Matters arising were dealt with, but Jude forbore to raise the question of the Chairmanship. In the heat of victory it had lost some of its urgency and he was inclined to feel that it was a problem time and distance would resolve. So the obstacles were despatched and the motion carried.

It was all over.

Everyone started talking at once. A burst of comradely laughter and the expression 'guillotine motion' reached my ears. Miss Makepeace, the elderly secretary Jude had inherited from his father, closed the minute book and dabbed at the corner of her eye while bottles and glasses were produced. Toasts were bandied back and forth. Champagne sparkled and spilled on the mahogany table. The bright globules magnified its grain.

I felt it was someone else who joined the jubilation, not me. I could see that Eudora was displeased and was taking her defeat with bad grace. As soon as she could, she summoned her chauffeur and left. Jude excused himself and went after her into the street, hoping to pacify her by inviting her to lunch, but by the time he caught up with her, she was ensconced in her seat and totally ignored him. He was left gesticulating through the glass as the car began to slide downhill to the bypass.

"Well, Angel," Neil Porteous laughed, "your husband certainly isn't one to let the grass grow under his feet!" The observation was touched with a searching, half-intimate compassion.

I looked into his sane and friendly freckled face with gratitude. "No," I agreed, and a vision came to me of the lawn at home complicated with trefoil and throngs of winking daisies which defied all attempts to banish them. "Perhaps that's why it's always greener elsewhere."

From then on, events cascaded and life began to dismantle itself around us. In view of my own drastic misgivings, I had not expected us to sail with the wind.

In the summer, the cottage was sold. The agents came and pasted a notice over the board to say so. I stared at the large vivid letters, the triumph and defeat of them. When I glanced outside quickly, I could have sworn that the word was in fact SOLID and wondered if it were some kind of valuation. So the comings and goings of the last few weeks with their air of theatrical unreality, the conducted tours of the interior, had culminated in this. A sale.

I busied myself packing clothes and crockery and books, frantically stuffing baby clothes into opaque carrier bags where they couldn't be seen. I'd leave them on the doorstep for the Scouts' Rummage Sale, then I wouldn't have to face parting with them. A flier had dropped through the letterbox advertising that a collection was to be made in the area that week. They could have the wicker cradle, too. No, they couldn't, because Jude would have to know. Well, the attic at the new house was big enough; the cradle could be stowed away, out of sight, along with all the other painful reminders, forgotten. "What about the nursery?" Jude had asked after I'd chosen wallpaper for all the main rooms from unwieldy books of samples he had brought home.

"Oh, time for that later," I said lightly and got on twice as fast with what had to be done in order to spare him needless work and worry. For I had never in my life been accustomed to lie. *Never.*

One by one the pictures came down. Barren spaces were stencilled in the grime on the walls. Next I removed the photographs and ornaments from the mantelpiece and alcoves and wrapped them carefully in tissue and newspaper and laid them in packing cases, filling every corner. The rooms had a forlorn and strangely closed-in look. The emptiness resounded and amplified the ticking of the clock. My cooking pans clashed like cymbals. You don't realise how much noise is softened by the fabric of day to day living. All the boxes were packed to bursting.

It occurred to me that maybe if I had told the truth, I wouldn't have had to go through any of this.

September rain filled the hollows gouged out of the drive by the furniture van yesterday afternoon. We spent our last night in Leicestershire with neighbours.

"All set and ready to go," Jude announced from the doorway, brushing the wet from his shoulders. Voices boomed, every footstep echoed. This was it, then. We were off. All that remained to be done was to leave the keys at the agent's office. Today someone else would take possession. The house would present some other facet of its character and would mould other destinies.

I couldn't understand why, having reached that point, I felt so little. It occurred to me that the meaning of mortality was severance, isolation, a cutting of umbilical cords.

Jude came to the window, infected a little with my mood. He put an arm around my shoulders and squeezed them tightly. "You made a wonderful home of this place," he said, "but you'll do it again. It's been a good foothold."

A foothold. I had thought it was for ever, this earth, these trees, that what we had planted would thrive here. What we had sown we would reap.

"I just want to remember…before we go…" I said and fell silent. I want to remember the way the sun slants through the window in the early morning, the way the birdbath makes rainbows shiver on the ceiling. I want to remember the wind in the poplars, how it whispers through their ephemeral silver with the sound of the sea. I want to remember the black cracks made in the night by the winter trees, as though the chasm itself were solid, palpable as stepping stones, and the way my star fixes itself in the forked tip of the bough; a germ of daylight, a promise.

"You won't forget," he told me. "You've a photographic memory. That will survive what you leave behind."

"Will it? Do you think it will?" I picked up my beaker from the windowsill to finish my drink. Coffee was dripping on to my hand. But when I looked down, feeling for a tissue, I saw that the fluid was strangely distilled, as clear as tears. "It's like in *The Cherry Orchard*, isn't it? It's not a bad idea that Russian custom of sitting down to reflect and collect oneself before a journey."

"Only we've nowhere to sit. Good grief! It's after nine. We must be off!"

"They've forecast storms on the radio, did you know?"

"Never," Jude said, locking the door. "It's not hot enough. It'll be even cooler further north. It'll be autumn there now, in Scotland."

We got into the car. Jude was beaming all over his face as he switched on the ignition. We were about to hit the trail at last! I felt his sinews flex with an urge to communicate exhilaration as he gave me another quick hug. The car moved forward, rolling over the gravel, and out of the drive. He braked and jumped out to close the gate. I heard it swinging to, the latch crashed home with a metallic thud. The cobwebs spun between its spars trembled and shed diamond drops.

Thin blue fumes came up from the exhaust. I did not look back. Spring, summer, the onset of autumn, what had led up to this moment fell away behind us. Ahead was winter in Scotland.

The car swung out into the road and gathered speed.

We were on the way.

# Afternoon

*He showed me lilies for my hair,*
*And blushing roses for my brow,*
*He led me through his gardens fair*
*Where all his golden pleasures grow.*

# Afternoon

"It'll be fine when we get there! You see!"

I smiled because this was what Jude always told me. The odd thing was that he was usually right, though it was hard to share his ingenuous faith at times.

The road to Scotland was a wide modern road. Heavens, he could remember the tortuous route of the old days, adding hours of travelling, the hair-raising gradients and bends which had made his caravan snake in a perilous fashion. "You'd to go all round the houses in those days. There was no other way."

Many scenes flashed past and were gone. To the right and the left one could glimpse other worlds. Once my eye stretched as far as the sea where sulphurous towns elbowed their way to the shore. Yes, there was tarnished air, but there was also air of pure oxygen engulfing lucid greens and blues, naked peaks and planes of satin water, regions one longed to explore, given time.

*Take me home, country roads* came over the radio as the car swept past the Border and left the tangle of motorways behind. We'd soon be there! Though it seemed that the fringes of this Promised Land, contiguous with the one we'd forsaken, were parched and sallow, even scrubby. Shaggy cattle lumbered about in open pasture, stopping now and then to fix ruminant eyes on the distance. A thin rain fell.

But sure enough, when we reached Glenfinnie and turned into the long twisting approach to our new home, the sky was aglow with a setting sun. Trees flickered past in the burning light. "You were right," I said.

Amused, he turned to say something but changed his mind. "You look tired. Your eyes are dark as bruises."

"Look! There's a lamp in one of the windows!"

"Good old Mrs Craig," Jude enthused. "She'll have seen to everything."

Mrs Craig was the bustling capable soul who 'did' for Mr Oliphant, the Minister. She had been good enough to let in the furniture removers and sign the delivery sheets. Both perched halfway up Linden Hill overlooking the little granite town, the Manse was the villa's sole neighbour.

The sight greeting us made us stand and stare. The vast oaken fireplace was not the gaping sepulchre it had been before. A fire crackled in the hearth, dancing flames lighting a constellation of sparks low in the chimney. The room was sweet with burnt maplewood, its shadows soft and mobile; friendly shadows. By the window, a table was half-spread with a linen cloth and a meal of chicken salad, rolls, peaches and cheese, awaited us.

Mrs Craig appeared from the kitchen in a blue gingham pinafore, her iron-grey hair done up in a coil. Her skin was grained like fine Morocco leather and her kindly eyes took you in at a glance. She had been a widow for many a long year, for her man had died overseas in the War and, having no bairns of her own, her life had been spent caring for other folk instead. There was no icon of the Blessed Virgin on the wall, but her presence was palpable.

"What a welcome!" Jude beamed. "You've gone to a lot of trouble."

"Well," said she, "if the house isn't all trig and trim, there's a fair spread to sit down to."

"It *is* good of you," I said. I was light-headed with relief, for I had imagined a house with no welcome at all, forgotten in stillness and shade behind its palisade of firs. Who could have foreseen such a banquet?

"I'll away now, for His Nibs has company and they'll be wanting their supper by and by. I'll look in later to make sure nothing's needed."

When we'd eaten, we explored the house, spellbound, seeing our own goods and chattels, left at random, mostly in the appropriate rooms. The floors were already carpeted, some new, scuffing fluff, and the walls papered with recognisable designs from the Harmony stable. Jude had been anxious to get the cracks covered before we moved in. In a flash, I saw how it might all come together as it had done before, the elements assembling in masterly co-ordination; curve echoing tendril and curve in wood and fabric, gilt fittings and paper.

"But the rooms are so large," I said aghast. "I'd forgotten how large they were. What we have will be lost in these spaces."

"We're not used to spreading ourselves. We shall need to go on adding to the furniture as time goes by and our pocket allows."

So it was not to be a renunciation, then, but a going on. A kind of adventure.

"I think I'll have an early night," I said. "I'm exhausted."

"Yes, why don't you? I'll start unpacking."

Mrs Craig, when she came, insisted she'd be the one to see to things and delved into a chest, drew out linen and blankets, sent them, folds flying, across the divan. I protested my gratitude in some confusion. "There, lassie, away to your bed now. You've a touch of fever, I reckon. I'll bring hot milk and a wee dram presently. Mr Oliphant's a meikle supply. Tis the juice of the barley keeps himself in fine fettle!"

At last I slipped thankfully between cool sheets but rest did not steady my erratic breathing. After the toddy, I dozed and slept. Then, all of a sudden, I started awake and didn't know what had caused it. Perhaps it was Jude coming upstairs. I'd been dimly aware of his movements below and the hum of cross-chat with Mrs Craig, the cadences, rising, falling. Or perhaps it was an impulse inside my own head. I became aware of the unfamiliar room and couldn't recall where the door was.

And then it took hold of me, despair of the deepest dye, and I wondered what dreadful aberration had brought me here, what madness had I abandoned myself to? It must be a dream, a side-track, a parenthesis, it could not be life, my life. What was I to do in that disarranged place, how retrieve what was lost? I climbed out of bed and went to the window, the sleep gone from my body. But the night sky was not my sky, nor the felt-black jaws of the horizon beyond. In the churchyard, the Celtic wheelcrosses loomed out like a battalion of advancing warriors. Grasses flowed beneath the blade of a sickle moon.

"You should be resting," coaxed a familiar voice as the light went on. "Why aren't you?"

I turned my face into the bedclothes to stifle my sobs, but they only grew worse. I wept and cried: "Take me home! Take me back! We don't belong here! We should never have come!"

I was usually so composed, so equal to any situation, whatever it cost. Jude had come to take that for granted. I might go so far as to say it was the bedrock of all he built. He was unnerved by the irrational strain in my voice. He tried to comfort me but though he said the right things, no power came from the words. This failure of the reflex of giving and taking, borrowing and lending, was beginning to confirm us in our separate ways.

"Look, you're tired and upset by the upheaval. Tomorrow everything will look different."

"Tomorrow...?" Tomorrow was a foreign country.

"Soon we shall feel we've always lived here. This is the house where we shall make all our memories. We'll bring up our children here…"

I detached from him, in the grip of shock. "But… it's… it's all been a hideous mistake!"

His voice rose a fifth. "I don't understand you! I don't know what it is you *do* want! You raved about Scotland. We had a fantastic time here. Neither of us wanted to go back."

"I sometimes think that hell, because of its very nature, must be on the outskirts of heaven, in full view of it. Eternal proximity, eternal division."

"Hell! Nobody believes in that guff nowadays. It's a relic of the Dark Ages. Mere cant to keep the masses in order! The trouble with you is, you spend too much time *thinking*."

"Why, why did you have to rush your fences so?"

"You know why. You can't dither in business. You strike while the iron's hot. Besides," he added in a voice stiff with acrimony, "I was brought up to temper my enthusiasm. Angus put the clamps on everything."

"Oh, Jude. You're tilting with a spectre. Why do you still have to win?"


In the night, in the first lone darkness of that uncharted place, when the blood pumped and whined in my ears, I was filled with remorse. I wanted to shake him and wake him and cry: *I will go with you. Don't leave me behind!*

Jude slept with his back turned inexorably upon me, sleeping the sleep of the just. Never, he was persuaded, could he be convicted of sacrificing anyone's peace of mind to his pride. He had done what was right, what was best.

In the past, we would have turned to one another and made amends, welded together so that we became what we had opposed and all things were made new. Love had been a self-perpetuating thing, recharging us with energy to remake the world. Now, I leased him my body, for that was all he seemed to want, the material part of me. He inspired no more, I gave no more, but endured acute guilt for the treachery of emptiness within. I told myself that it was inevitable, this parting of the ways, love-making belonged to life and I did not. But it didn't dislodge the guilt.


No sooner had the house been put in reasonable order with the help of Harmony's chief chemist than Jude was itching to be back on the treadmill.

He worked long hours, regularly staying away until eight or nine in the evening. Each morning, I watched his car strike out on the highway and absorb itself into the flow of life and purpose. Turning back into the illimitable spaces of the house, I felt struck out by the shrillest pitch of silence. It was the worst time of all. I would grip a table or chair, the doorhandle, anything that claimed existence in the objective world. I could have sworn that it shrank from my touch.

What could I, having one foot in the next world, have in common with others now?

How could I share their motive force, their aims? All my senses were becoming attuned to another dimension. Everywhere I saw evidence of chaos and corruption, as if death were creeping through the widening interstices of life. It came like the slow awakening of maturity through the turbulent years of adolescence. I passed people on street corners locked together in collusion, holding the kind dialogue that would forever exclude me. I marvelled at the facility with which topics were introduced. Often I had to struggle to make an approach for what I wanted to say, otherwise the lines of communication got crossed. But others did not appear to have this handicap. At least, if they did, it didn't bother them. They didn't notice.

And then it dawned on me, as I listened more intently, that the dialogues were not dialogues at all, but merely monologues interleaving. No thread of sympathy held them together, no common focal point. Nevertheless upon one subject there seemed to be agreement and that was the high cost of living. They coalesced between the aisles of the supermarket, a murder of crows around carrion, cramming wire baskets with offers, overspending in order to save, striving to get a purchase on inflation. The devalued currency changed hands. It was everyone for himself.

For economy, or the lack of it, was at the root of every problem, it seemed to me then. So frustrated had we become by its tyranny that we had started wishing for the moon. People ran amok throughout the earth, tearing themselves from their roots, spilling over boundaries, plundering one another's land so that black was white and white black. All those dark faces mottling the streets of Europe were surely not despised and resented for themselves. It was because they bore witness to greed and a love of gain. They were blots on the northern conscience. Deep down the fair-skinned races feared they might be persecuted and overrun by the evil they themselves had unleashed.

I was dispersing a mound of laundry, flinging the items into their respective piles, when these thoughts went racing through my head. I was on the point, the very point, of solving some mystery deep within.

At last it came to me, the truth, clear as crystal, as I was closing the door of the machine. The light came on; I heard the running of water in dry places. Love of gain and fear of death were one and the same!

Of course, it had been such an advantage that they could both speak the same language, Jude thought, as he shook hands warmly with Carlo Serafini on the forecourt of the Elgin Hotel. Interpreters were a bind and destroyed the essential camaraderie of the thing. Besides the annoyingly protracted exchanges, there was always the danger that a wrong construction might be placed on an idiomatic phrase, or a little concession lost. Jude's knowledge of Italian barely covered the common courtesies.

The Armani-suited Milanese imparted a slick elegance to every gesture. Even his hired car seemed to fit him like a slipper as he coaxed its throaty engine to life, the hot stench of exhaust fumes filling the darkness.

It had been raining and the tarmac was awash with borrowed radiance from the foyer. A limousine was drawing up at the door to disgorge passengers clad in their evening finery. Voices carried. A gale of distant laughter echoed around the walls and archways. Jude unlocked his car and flung his brief-case on to the rear seat, inhaling deeply. He had clinched a very satisfactory deal. A foot in the door with the Crespi group could lead to bigger things. The sky was the limit.

He glanced up at a black eternity bristling with stars, suddenly oppressed by having to return to Linden Hill and Angel in no mood to be swept off her feet by his news. Perhaps he'd go into the hotel and have just one drink before driving back.

The bar was crowded. People were clustered in congenial groups, chattering with remarkable energy and dedication. Gas jets flamed around imitation logs under a copper cowl in the middle of the room, as mesmerising as a real fire. No one appeared to be at a loose end. He sidled through the scrum, carefully piloting his drink, and drifted into the spacious vestibule, lavishly glazed, where he could watch the taxis coming and going, the red brake lights punctuating the dazzling reflections on the pane. He felt more at home there among the potted ferns and fleecy pampas grasses.

Before long, he realised that he was being observed through the medium of a long mirror. At first he thought it a trick of fancy, but then he knew it wasn't. The woman's eyes vacillated between him and the paperback she was holding. It was one of the grey Penguin Modern Classics he had once picked out on Angel's shelves, a Camus entitled *The Outsider*, the disturbing story of a man for whom there is no reality but an objective one. He recognised the figure on the cover, the harrowing geometry of its sightless face, painted no doubt by some Cubist brush to convey primitive truth when war had done its utmost to strip away culture. The woman, somewhere in her late thirties or early forties, was dressed entirely in black, her classic silk shirt unfastened by three buttons at the top and her classic skirt modestly slit at the bottom. She was wearing, he noticed, a small silver crucifix. Apart from a faint trace of lipstick, her flawless skin was devoid of any obvious make-up, but there was something distinctly profligate in the convex of her brow and her high cheekbones. She had about her the look of a consummate self-deceiver, at once furtive and complacent.

Lord, he thought, flushing warmly around the gills, she's got me salted! In an establishment of this kind, too! She wouldn't dare to come here more than a couple of times a year in case she was spotted and hustled away by the management. A professional lady on display to keen-eyed professional gentlemen. The conference facilities were fully booked. He wondered whether she was one of those liberated females campaigning for recognition of her services. The 'black economy' with a vengeance, he mused. Still, some theorists claimed it was what kept the country afloat!

He rose and jostled his way to the bar where he became involved in a discussion with the barman about the dry summer in Scotland and its effect upon angling and the tourist trade. He suspected he was stalling for time, leaving space of an answer to an unidentified problem. Returning to the vestibule some fifteen minutes later, he was in time to see the lift doors narrow on the spectacle of the woman escorted by a portly guy with a beard. The gap closed silently.

It seemed colder than ever outside. Frost had begun to sparkle thinly on the car roofs. The roads would be dicey. He was fumbling with his keys, trying to jam the wrong one into the lock, when some shadowy movement against the hedge, captured momentarily in the swinging beam of a pair of headlights, caught his eye. A dodgem-like Fiat was parked there. Its owner had succeeded in jacking up the vehicle and changing the wheel, but was having trouble tightening the bolts. It soon became plain that the resourceful mechanic was female.

"I bet Emmeline Pankhurst didn't tie herself to the railings for that. Here, let me give you a hand."

"You'll need both," she said. "I know how a man can be trusted to put a spanner in the works."

"*Touché.*"

"A lucky thing I made it to the hootel when the tyre gave out. I wouldnae fancy tackling this in heavy traffic."

She focused the fading rays of her torch for him. Clearly, she said, it wasn't her day. There had been an unpleasant scene with her ailing stepfather who, after many years of indifference towards her, expected her to 'come home' and minister to him. As it was, she had taken an agency job, the better to arrange leave in an emergency. "I've my own flat and a few savings put by," she told Jude. "I've worked hard to get it, I'll not let it go."

"No, indeed," he replied, wincing with the effort of forcing the spanner around its last revolution. "I can't say I blame you."

She went on to explain that her boyfriend was a waiter at the Elgin and it should have been his night off. She had turned up to collect him, since his own car was in dock, only to learn that he was having to cover for a sick colleague. "To be honest," she said, "he's been away all the summer season in Scandinavia and the relationship's wearing a bit thin."

Jude pulled himself up and rubbed his hands on his handkerchief, the hubcap replaced. The keys chinked in his pocket. The girl thanked him profusely. He could see that she was not unattractive, abundant Pre-Raphaelite hair the colour of terracotta framing a heart-shaped face appealingly streaked with grime.

Upstairs in the ballroom, the band wound up *Toujours Fidele* and launched without pausing into *Strangers In The Night*. "Look, why don't you let me buy you a drink?"

"Och, fine," she said, "but I oughtae buy you one. I'll away and get clean and tidy first, though."

She emerged from the Powder Room extracting a purse from the assortment of curiosities in her tote bag.

"I'll get them," Jude insisted. "You must allow a mere male some privileges."

She grinned. "Mine's Perrier Water."

"Are you sure?"

"Aye," she said. "Alcohol dries the complexion and shrivels the liver! I'm into healthy eating and antioxidants."

"Ah, detoxification. Prefer *in*toxicants myself."

"You should look after yoursel'. You're all you've got!"

"Well, perhaps I will join you in a mineral water. I've already downed a couple of shots and I'm driving back to Glenfinnie tonight." Home seemed a long way off, like looking through the wrong end of a telescope.

"You've a wife and bairns waiting?" the girl quizzed when he returned with the drinks.

"No. No children, that is. Angel – my wife – lost a baby last winter. She's since been very depressed."

"Och, there'll be more, maybe."

"I doubt it," he replied in an undertone, surprised at the bitterness in his own voice. The frustration swelled intolerably under his breastbone.

"I thought o' gett'n wed once," the girl reflected, as though it was a decision to be reached in isolation, "but I value my independence."

"And what exactly do you do?"

"I'm a Temp secretary," she told him. "It has it's advantages, moving around, but I'd prefair something more perrmanent. Incidentally, I'm Marilyn McIvor. Friends call me Marnie. Who are you?"

Jude apologised for having overlooked the matter of an introduction. He could only think it was because he was at ease. Squinting down the interior pocket of his jacket, he produced a business card which he handed to Marnie with a flourish. "Call me," he said. "I'm looking for someone like you."


She was sporting the same red tartan cape and Tam O' Shanter to match when she walked into Jude's office during the lunch break next day to find him hammering upon an ancient typewriter that looked as though it belonged in a car boot sale. His tie was loose and his shirt collar open in harassed executive mode. He was preparing a speech he had rashly undertaken at short notice to deliver at a dinner that evening. The firm's progress chart on the wall behind him described an impossible diagonal from the bottom left to the top right hand corner.

"That must be one Noah chucked out," she greeted him.

He was startled by her arrival from nowhere. "*You* haven't wasted any time."

"There was no one in Reception. The door was open, so I came right in."

"They're all in The Taverners' Arms."

"And are you pollut'n your innards wi' that?" she demanded, indicating the remains of some fudge-filled confection on the windowsill. It's loaded with theobromine."

"Ah, the god Chocolate! Opiate of the starving slave-driven."

"A racehorse failed the dope test recently after snatching one o' thoose from a stable lad!" she informed him.

Marnie withdrew from her bag a transparent box filled with mayonnaise and beansprout sandwiches. She offered one to Jude and then took one herself which she proceeded to munch with considerable relish perched on the edge of his desk.

"My," she said, observing the wallchart, "you're going places fast."

"That's *broadly* the picture," Jude said with a sheepish grin. "A compromising sawtooth line, albeit on a general ascendant, might not inspire quite the same faith with the bank."

"You're a canny one."

"So rumour has it. These sandwiches are pretty good."

She shoved the box towards him, taking stock of his disordered lair, the heaped abeyance tray and the expanding volumes of screwed up paper in the bin. "It's plain tae see, though, you're in sore need of Ms Fixit."

"Well, Miss er..." Jude couldn't remember which clan she belonged to.

"*Ms*," she corrected, "McIvor."

"Ah, your manifest independence."

"Aye, that," she cautioned regarding him with a minatory eye.

"Well, you'd best make a start. I'll send the Temp packing this very p.m."

"Not withoot a few concessions to technology!"

"Fear not. There's a nervous six-cylinder thing that spits when you breath on it. Churns out stuff in a jiffy."

"But you havenae given me an interview!"

"I think we might safely dispense with the formalities, Ms McIvor. You've already supplied your *curriculum vitae*!

An hour later, he collected his papers together and slipped them into a drawer. As he did so, he came across an oval-framed photograph of Angel, taken unawares on their honeymoon, for which there seemed to be no convenient situation in the new office, and was visited by an alarming sensation of having done something lunatic.

"The *home keys*, "Marilyn McIvor had pointed out, tut-tutting over the indecipherable passages of his speech when he complained that the blasted typewriter was suffering from dyslexia. "It'll no come out right till you mind the *home keys*. It'll no make any kindae sense."

*"Seek first the Kingdom... and all these things will be given to you."*

Often, my thoughts returned to childhood, for life had gained a reshuffled chronology. Those days were closer now than they had been in the intervening years. The past, my own past and the world's, was not a husk which had been discarded, it was yet alive, being continually revived in the present, forming the flesh and bone of a new generation, presenting the same signposts. My mind flew back to that signal day in my seventh year when reality was black and white and a fledgling came to grief mistaking a reflection for the real thing.

Ah, there was wisdom in children that they dug in their own back yards for buried treasure. I remembered how we had trooped to the historic chapel of Our Lady of Sorrows, two by two, each Sunday, we orphans, and had sat in serried rows, and how cool it was, even in summer. Yet I liked the stone-chilled mustiness of the place. I liked the choral responses striking in the spectral beams shafting through the fruit-drop windows. They reverberated on another plane altogether and my shivers were not of cold, but of excitement as if I grasped that through the discipline of symbolic ritual one could be conducted to some profound and longed-for state. We were an embodied people, like the Chosen Race. There in the presence of outsiders, beneath the indulgent gaze of elders and old ladies, I experienced a sense of belonging that was never achieved in the Home itself, though Fr. Hope, our chaplain, often spoke of it as being 'one big happy family'. 'Suffer little children to come unto Me, and forbid them not: for of such is the Kingdom of Heaven," Msgr. Fitzgerald quoted from the gospels. He would look benignly upon us, over the top of his half-moon spectacles, and I felt proud to be numbered with those who had come into their own. There was another text I associated with this one, though I couldn't fit it to any occasion. 'Except a man be born again, he cannot see the Kingdom of God'.

It seemed fair this, a piece of Divine Justice, that there should be a second chance. The next time round we might have fathers and mothers, a cottage with shutters and a bright red front door. Beyond, there would be open meadows where dandelions grew. The fading tufts would evolve into diaphanous circles, frailer than a candle's halo, and you could blow away to your heart's content and not care whether the time arrived at was the real time of day at all. No bells, no prayers, no orderly queues to calibrate the day, no shoe inspections, shines that obscured cramped toes, no shoulders chipped in narrow corridors. In the meadow there would be space. There would be hedgerows barbed with thorns to protect the families of young birds.

I can't say I was conscious of deprivation as a child. Yet during pregnancy, I realised how ill-equipped I was for motherhood. What pattern was there to conform to? I was not unaware of some guiding and protective hand behind the scenes, but God as my Father, and Holy Mary as my Mother, seemed a little remote. Jesus as my Elder Brother was perhaps more accessible. He was on a par, someone I could run to when bruised by my own mortality since he seemed to have a soft spot for his siblings. We took it all on trust, we children, heard Mass said on our behalf, until such time as the tenets of Catholic teaching came 'live' for us after Confirmation.

I took for granted that I understood what it all meant. But only now, facing a blank wall, did the mystery truly begin to deliver its charge. I saw the possibility of a new heaven and a new earth, New Jerusalem, with an inner vision like the radiance contained within the prism of a crystal. A new premium was assigned to every aspect of *being* so that people, concepts, objects appeared in a re-arranged relationship to one another. There was a new goal to aim for, a new measuring stick which suffered no alteration at the whim of Governments, Economic Communities and the mores of the day.

I began to see that life and death existed in symbiosis.


It was only then that I longed for fresh air and wide open spaces. Through a back window, one fine morning, I beheld heather drenched in a silvery mantle of dew that took hours to evaporate, and later that day, struck out across it. It was safer, now, outside. I didn't have to recruit all my strength as a defence against life.

But as soon as forest vapours piqued the senses and music sounded deep in the throat of the babbling burn, pictures of the past came reeling back. This was where we had been so happy, Jude and I. He paused again and again to shutter scenes for all he was worth. He had picked foxgloves for me, and bell heather (illegally, I think!) One day we went fishing on a borrowed permit and spent the whole day by the loch. I danced barefoot across the boulders, the water sluicing around each stony island, and Jude got a snapshot of me suspended forever in mid-air! He took another of me perched on an upturned boat. I was singing, I remember, Gaelic folk ballads. In the distance, the mountains were perfectly rendered, delicate as chipped shells sweeping up to the sky and bathed in a gold and iridescent light.

"The air is so clear here," Jude said, rapt. "Everything's in harmony." I thought: *But wars are waged for this, men die. Regimes are overthrown, kings sent to the scaffold, men of letters into exile, leaders assassinated so that the streets run with blood. Women have chained themselves to railings like martyrs about to be burnt at the stake, children have been sacrificed to idols. Monoliths have been hewn from the mountain's core and temples erected close to the heavens in improbable places. For this, deserts have been crossed and impenetrable surfaces mined. For this, Jerusalem itself is riven by war and holy doctrine, and some maintain that even the Garden of Eden has a geographic location. For this. For what is abstract and God's image in the heart of Man.*

Comparing those days with the present, I saw how locked Jude had become in his own solipsist universe and how a gulf had opened up between us. Partly I was to blame for having withdrawn as a means of self-protection. But there was that other factor, his restless quest to possess, which time and circumstance failed to fulfil.

Yet out of my despair a new comfort was born. I asked myself why he had chosen this rock on which to establish his kingdom. Surely not because his grandmother was a pennypinching Strachan, she who'd inculcated the traits he'd so despised and fought in Angus. "A tartar she was and no mistake," he would say. "Saved everything down to pieces of string to make ends meet!"

True, he was proud of his ancestral link with Scotland and felt himself woven in with the warp and weft of its lore, kindled readily to its abrasive wit. But it was not until we went scaling the Grampian foothills, beneath china-blue skies, that he saw the future unfurling and began to speak of development sites.

Maybe that was the one true point of polarisation in his life and, in going back, he was seeking his way again.

I reached the road where the burn issued into a hollow underneath and sang down into the glen, tumbling over itself in its rush to be united with the ocean, and bending down, let the water trickle through my fingers. Its purling ropes twisted this way and that, splitting strands over the earth's uneven surface. Collisions, collusions, a glad rushing together, inevitable partings. Where was the Jude I had once loved so passionately? And where, too, was the girl he had loved in return? I had begun to accept that there was to be a parting of the ways, but not this. I had seen Jude striding into the future and myself cut off, but not this. Whether I lived for a month or a year or a normal life's span was of no great account. It had precious little to do with the true parting of the ways which followed an admission of the part death played in the scheme of things. Was I, then, the one who was going on? He who was being left behind to squander his energies on a merry-go-round, getting nowhere fast?

I scrambled back up the bank between clumps of feathery brown bracken, moisture squeezing from the turf beneath my feet. A pressure of tears under my breastbone. And still the isolation, familiar as toothache.

The wind bit through my clothes. I turned up my collar resolutely. I would go back through the town and people would see me and I should see them.


Glenfinnie town buzzed like a hive at the close of the day's transactions. Smoke spiralled from chimneys and windows deflected rinsed light. The air smelled damp, of fermenting leaves and the chemistry of resurrection begun. Folk moved about as if they knew where they were going and what they had to do. An aroma of oatcakes and newly-risen dough wafted from The Gilded Cage tea shop in the High Street, whose blazing hearth threw back a rosy glow on the antique profiles and feeble joints of its patrons. There was a sense of going to ground for the winter.

Passing Goodfellow's bookshop, exhibiting the work of a local artist, I thought of the pictures still to be painted. I'd set to work soon. Behind its bow window a shadowy presence moved to the door and switched round the sign from Open to Closed. Barely I saw him, but I smiled, for he was a companion in my happiness, never mind how brief and remote the encounter or that his door was bolted against the world until nine in the morning.

Further along, going out of the town past the terraced cottages, I came upon Fairlie's farm and Fairlie himself, a canny stock, they said, slicing through timber as though it were butter with a chainsaw. The blond logs were quartered and stacked by the byre. He nodded and pushed back his cap with his thumb. "A keen wind," he called, "and if I'm any judge a coarse winter to come."

"Never mind," I chuckled, "when the spring comes we shall feel it is bought and paid for."

But he, Scots to the core, didnae care for that!


So that evening it was not only Jude who came in fresh from the world with other atmospheres about his bearing. I, too, crossed the threshold from the other side.

He was nothing if not taken aback that I was there to meet him at the door, so accustomed had he grown to a muted welcome and the grind of changing down to a lower gear when all he wanted was food and a remission from the cares of the day. He acted almost like a trespasser in his own house.

"I'm sorry," I said, seeing his gaze fall on empty plates and nothing happening in the kitchen. "I've been out."

"Oh? Well, I'm glad. You look better for it. Where did you get to?"

"To the bridge, by Cairn's croft. I came back a different way."

"You'll have come through the town, then."

"Yes, it's quite a long haul."

I looked at him, proud of my achievement and pleased to deliver such a gift, but he made no comment, only strode to the drinks cabinet and switched on the News. I think I must have hovered a little too expectantly, for he said: "Tomorrow we'll go out together. I'll take you somewhere for dinner. How's that?"

The evening slipped away in a series of silences, behind newspapers, over mended seams and in front of the television. Halfway through a flickering saga of an oil-strike succeeding against great odds, I was spent. "I think I'll hit the sack," I said.

An hour later, when Jude came up, I was still awake, but the light was out. I lay with my back to him, struggling to control my breathing and my hammering heart. If only I could sink into drowsiness, forget. It was far harder to lie down, a discipline, than to occupy myself with tasks to match my restlessness until my energy overstretched itself and got deeper and deeper into debt. He loosened his belt and undressed in a wedge of light from the landing. The buckle jangled. His clothes made a silvery rasping sound against his skin. The bed heaved as be got in beside me. I caught at the covers hardly knowing whether the landslide was inside my own head or out there from his imperative weight. I let go, but he was kissing me intently, my hair, my mouth, drawing the strappy nightgown away from my shoulders. "Angie, I want you. Oh God, I want you." And, of course, I had known it would be this way. He would catch at that glimmer of life in me, a man of keen passions ground down with the bearing of them, denied again and again with my soft 'tomorrow'. Outwardly he was not rough exactly, but I felt him tower above me in a white intensity of strength, effacing me, off on some erratic course of his own. I could not *absorb* him. I could lend him no momentum nor espouse such deranged rhythms, if rhythms they were. I tried, quailed, rose up, failed. I would surely break apart with this divisive force, its tension mounting. He trembled and seized upon his private zenith, letting his captive loose.

I escaped from him, panting, choking, and hid my face in the pillow, banished to the same wilderness as he. I was being punished for bringing him to where he had no wish to be. It was as if he must justify, at my expense, the path he had chosen. Or perish.

Afterwards, there was no sense of well-being, no veins scoured clean by the universal tide. How often in the past we had tumbled together again in the night, finding    redoubled    pleasure,    nothing    forfeited, something gained, in the repetition. He reached out for my hand, but I flinched in wild alarm. For this was not Jude. Not the husband to whom I'd drawn close when I couldn't settle at night, so that his electricity flowed into me, my pulse steadied, adopting the metre of his, and I slept. My eye was drawn to the silhouette of the half-open door, the strip of light broken at the hinges and the room passing by degrees into darkness. It was an alien presence slumped there beside me, depleting the air of oxygen. There was an 'otherness' about him I didn't recognise.

It took me a while to tumble to the truth.

"...*Assuring you of our best attention at all times. Yours faithfully,*" Jude ended a lengthy stint of dictation the following morning, all this thoughts reduced to the scrappy symbols covering the pages of Marilyn's notebook. "That should keep you nicely occupied until lunchtime." It was half past noon.

"Incidentally, you havenae replied to that invitation yet."

"Which would that be?"

"The Energy Conference at Edinburgh University. It's on Thursday and Friday the week after next. You are free."

Jude swivelled upon his chair, scrutinising the object gracing his desk which the manufacturers described as an 'executive toy'. It consisted of a free-swinging metal rod which, when set in motion, jerked crazily between different magnetic fields. He gave it a careless punch. "I suppose," he said, "that we ought to show willing."

"I agree. Consairvation's important if we're to have any future at all. It could be to our material advantage. Only yesterday, John was saying that our fuel consumption's too high."

"Oh, Meredith's always making noises about tightening our belts. He's forever turning down thermostats and switching off lights. It's what he *does*!"

"He also feels it might be a good idea to install our own generator."

Jude listened, his brows arched in amusement. It appeared he was not the only one who was developing a rapport with the new PA. What a contrast she was to Makepeace! He'd had to bear with that lady's complex efficiency for too long. Having been much attached to his father, she had been inclined to regard Jude as an upstart junior with the maddening authority to disrupt her systems whenever the fancy took him, a legacy of her having once discovered him, as a boy in short trousers, pilfering humbugs from a tin in the safe.

The needle came to a halt in Marilyn's quarter, surrendering to the magnet's superior power.

"Since you feel so strongly about it, you'd best pack your PJs and come along too. Book us in at the Atholl Palace if you can."

"Two rooms at the Atholl Palace! *He'll* have a seizure," she declared, tossing her coppery head toward the Accountant's office.

"At least we aren't called upon to endure the spartan conditions of the campus in term time, thank God," Jude remarked. He began to peruse a report, screwing up his features in mock concentration. "And make it *two* rooms, if you must. What happened to Scottish thrift?"


That afternoon Jude rang me to say he'd been detained at the office. Would I cancel our table at The Last Drop Inn?

"All right," I agreed, half-glad of the reprieve. "Some other time, perhaps."

Several evenings later, I sat and waited, dressed to go out, but Jude did not come. In the hall, the grandfather clock chimed eight; the pendulum launched into another lap. Silence reclaimed the house.

It was chilly in the drawing room. Pointless to light a fire and waste fuel when there would be nobody in. I hadn't the stamina for such tasks and had been saving my energy for the evening.

At twenty to nine, I got up from leafing through a magazine, my head swimming with fatigue, and parted the curtains. The night was starless. Over the town, the sky was tinged with a phosphorescent glow. What if Jude had had an accident? Surely he would have rung if he expected to be late. I was visited by a sudden, quite irrelevant vision of him that time in Norway: he was standing on the edge of a precipice, pointing out The Bridal Veil. The thought, once entertained, took hold. I picked up the phone and dialled the office. There was just a chance someone would still be there. Harmony had more work than could be handled at present.

At length a click snuffed out the ringing tone at the other end and introduced me to a gross emptiness. I heard a man's voice too far from the mouthpiece to be distinct.

"Jude?"

"Hello? Hello? Oh, it's you, Angie."

"Aren't you coming?"

"Coming?"

"We were going out, remember?"

He swore. He sounded mildly drunk, and I had the impression that he was not alone. "Babe, I'm *guttingly* sorry. I've been tied up all afternoon with a buyer. An important contract."

"You might have let me know!"

"I did. At least I tried to contact you earlier, but the line was dead. I meant to try again later. It seems all right now."

"Perhaps it's only the incoming calls that misfire."

"I've been on to the engineers, anyway. They're coming first thing in the morning."

"It's funny," I said, "the way we can't seem to synchronise our comings and goings these days," and rang off.

Jude loitered over the automatic shoebrush on the second floor of the Atholl Palace Hotel, uppers gleaming. A toothbrush was slotted into his breast pocket. About halfway down the corridor, a man came out of a room and the door slammed against him, echoing around the walls. Two other men ambled past with their hands behind their backs, deep in discussion about sales technique and the prevalence of palm-greasing. The swish and glide of lift doors; and Jude was alone again. His intention was to ambush the waiter bearing the champagne he had ordered for the unwitting occupant of Room 133. The Up and Down arrows above the lift kept lighting up and, presently, another ping announced the arrival of the Bollinger. A nod and a wink, not to mention a sweet tosheroon, and the waiter was soon persuaded that Jude could be relied upon to discharge the duty without a hitch.

So far so good.

Supporting the tray upon his arm, he rapped on the gilt and white door.

"Who is it?" Marnie called, vexed, uncertain.

"Room Service, madam. Your champagne. (Would she recognise his voice, despite the affected Cork brogue?)

The door opened cautiously, linked to the post by a chain. "But there's been a mistake. I didnae order…" She appeared in the narrow space looking, for all her singularity, rather vulnerable, having dragged a flannel robe hastily over a pair of plaid pyjamas trimmed with *broderie Anglaise*.

Jude gave a theatrical blink. "Hadrian was wasting his time...!"

Marnie's eyes flashed with indignation. "Away you go," she said firmly. "I'll no be need'n a nightcap, thank you."

"Oh, come on, Irondraws," he hissed, "you can't leave a fellow on the doorstep. What will people *think?*"

An elderly couple, walking by, raised their brows. He could hear the disgruntled tone of their comments some paces away.

The door banged. On the inside, the chain rattled gratifyingly. It opened again to admit him. Marilyn gave vent to forced sigh in which fury competed with exasperation. "Just what do you take me for?"

"A bottle of bubbly and a tip to Room Service so far!"

Jude uncorked the champagne and splashed it into the glasses, congratulating himself that the first hurdle was cleared.

"You're half-cut already, y'knoo that?"

"Cheers!"

She stood there, arms folded in female warrior mode. The significance of the toothbrush did not elude her. "Now will you hurry yoursel'. I'm tired and the answer's NOO!"

"That's good," Jude grinned, "because the question is: *You're not going to turf me out to spend the night in my own room, are you, when the bed's as hard as a pool table?"*

"I'm going to bed," she informed him, shedding her robe and climbing in. "Will you kindly put the tray out when you've finished and close the door *from the other side.*"

"You're a hard woman, Marnie."

"I make it a rule never tae get involved wi' married men," she said, pulling up the covers around her. "What about your poor wife? She needs you, I doon't."

"Actually, my wife doesn't need me. She doesn't need anyone. She lives the life of a recluse since we moved north. She gave up her job as an art teacher when we lost the baby and hasn't worked since. She immures herself in that house all day and I feel like a stranger walking in."

"She's taking time to adjust to the new environment. A bout of depression is no boost to confidence."

"It's her *domain*. I don't belong there."

"Is that her photograph in your drawer at the office?" Marnie probed. "She's a very attractive lady."

"She used to be so outgoing, so vivacious. She was orphaned as a baby, but, boy, did she know how to take the world on! Now she's someone else. It's as though her sights are trained on something I can't see." We've become foreigners to one another's shores, Jude thought, and unaccustomed to the rate of exchange. He snapped out of his abstraction to find himself being watched with pitying shrewdness. "I don't know why the hell I'm telling you all this. I didn't come here to discuss my wife."

He observed with some irritation the specimen of ultra-modern art above the headboard, a web of hallucinatory colours spun over a blackened ground.

"Why *did* you come?" Marnie asked.

A little later, after a fraternal peck, he made his way blearily back to his room, leaving the bottle upturned in the ice-bucket outside her door.


I began to sense that affairs at Harmony Wallcoverings were not running as smoothly as Jude had banked on. This made it even more vital to his self-esteem to win me back to the place we once occupied, he ready to lead, I to follow. I did not know how to convey that the old life would never be restored.

The night he was away in Edinburgh, I lay thinking about our adventures together. The places we'd been to, the sights we'd seen! It seemed impossible ever to have ached for his love, for the sheer joy of having my arms full of him, admitting him to every curve and convolution of my veins. Oh, to remember it took my breath away! The world was full of young lovers once, clasped in the lime-dappled shade of avenues, down Moorish alleys to which the sun referred obliquely at noon, along embankments in the lyric calm just off the beaten track. We ourselves, when we'd soaked up the culture, would be anxious to disclose the space between where we were and a hotel room, a *Do Not Disturb* notice in several languages strung up on the doorhandle.

He remembered those times, too. It was the yardstick he could not abandon. His Eden.

The garden at Linden Hill ran to seed. Jude hadn't the heart to tame the grass or uproot the multitudes of nettles. He'd make a start in the spring, slash the intertwined tendrils and wrench out the stubborn network of roots. He said that great forests were as down on the earth's surface compared to what went on underground.

When we were first getting a home together, he'd laboured to put the cottage garden in order, building rockeries, planting out beds, creating little pools to refresh the eye while sweat dripped from his brow, until the whole area broke into new relief. Now a kind of spiritual atrophy had overtaken him. Of course, knowing what had gone into that, I could understand that he was daunted at having to start all over again. I went out myself with a trowel and spade and clutched at the weeds, binding them around my fingers for extra purchase. Here and there a patch was cleared, bulbs pressed into the sifted soil, until my head pulsed and the tools fell from my grasp.

So the garden ran wild. The weeds flourished and sought to subjugate one another, each species bent on prevailing until the humblest were weakened by attenuation and the strongest gained ground. As Jude vanished and materialised between the dank trees, jangling the loose change deep in his pockets, I realised how the weeds had destroyed all sense of perspective. It was hard to imagine the garden there had been, or might be. Soon we should be hacking a path to get through at all.

"All those rooms," repined Eudora Brightman, "and no sign of a grandchild yet!"

"Barracks of a place," submitted the Colonel, absorbed in a copy of the *Financial Times* which he had propped up beside his plate whilst eagerly applying himself to grilled bacon and sausages. "Draughty, too. Not as cosy as your abode, m'dear."

They were breakfasting together at a table for two in the Cadogan Arms Hotel, fourteen miles south of Glenfinnie, having been taken the previous day on a conducted tour of what Jude was pleased to call 'the new complex' and afterwards for tea at Linden Hill. Eudora had staunchly declined an invitation to spend the night under her son's roof. Her displeasure was not to be lightly appeased, though she had endeavoured to preserve a fair degree of civility throughout the visit.

"I had a little chat with Angel."

"Nice girl. Fetching young filly. Looks tired."

"There was a distinct atmosphere of tension, did you notice?"

The Colonel bayoneted half a sausage and thrust it between his jaws, chewing mightily. "Made us very welcome, I thought. Good spread," he said, refusing to divert his focus.

"I suspect all is not well between those two."

"No solution to *The Times* dispute."

"Of course, I knew it wouldn't work," maintained Eudora with an air of sagacity. "I said so right from the start. I explained, oh so diplomatically, that she honestly wasn't fitted for the role of Managing Director's wife with all its social responsibilities. No family, no background, no *connections*. Unheard of in the County!"

"War between the Management and Unions hotting up."

"If you choose to make a fool of yourself and contract such an ill-starred marriage, I said, don't come running to me to put your house in order when things go awry. But he wouldn't listen. He was besotted with her. His head was quite turned."

Colonel Raven shook out the crackling pink pages of his newspaper and turned his attention to the share quotations. "Knew when he was on to a good thing, shouldn't wonder."

"Angus didn't approve of her, either, but the sly minx somehow won him over. In fact, to be absolutely candid," continued Eudora, warming to her theme, "there is no shadow of doubt in my mind that, irrespective of the line she takes, she is behind this latest flight of folly, urging Jude to prove what he is capable of under her regime."

"Minimum Lending Rate's through the roof. Allied Bonds in the doldrums. Might be the time to buy."

"What can she know of commercial operations? She hasn't the faintest notion how inflation *works*," persisted she, whose butcher, after many years of custom, had had sufficient compunction to point out that it really wasn't necessary to buy sirloin steak in order to make a casserole. She bit into a croissant spread with a prodigal layer of Elsenham grapefruit marmalade. "I am not a snob, never have been. It is against my principles. I like people of all kinds. Variety is the spice of life. But certain positions require a certain breeding, a certain *savoir faire*. Her head is full of Dali and Picasso."

"Rum cove, Picasso. No grasp of form. Made a pig's breakfast of the Spanish Civil War."

"*The Rubik's cube has a lot of answer for.*"

"Churchill's the feller."

"Churchill?"

"Chartwell. Tranquil landscapes. Keeps the Black Dog at bay."

"The Black Dog?"

"The glums, m'dear. Where's the use surrounding yourself with a bad trip at the front line?"

"It is all most unsatisfactory, most disappointing. This time I fear he'll have to pay for his wanton disregard of my opinion. He has bitten off more than he can chew." Eudora dabbed at the corners of her mouth with an impeccably laundered napkin.

"Should pull through," said the Colonel, folding his newspaper and taking out two antacid tablets which he crunched and swilled down with the dregs of his coffee. "Good staff. Strong team. Meredith's the man. Got his head screwed on. Know's what's what." Unlike that conceited ass of a son of yours, he mused. Young devil needed taking down a peg or two. A mischievous twinkle lit his gaze as he considered this for a moment. He sighed. He hated long excursions, even with a chauffeur, especially at this time of year. Always on edge away from home. Liked his feet to be under his own table, or preferably Eudora's. Dreary days with too much of a nip in 'em. Nothing doing at Lord's or The Oval for months on end. Long dark nights. Couldn't sleep for the burning pain in his lower limbs which no liniment would soothe. Thought of the fleecy underblankets Eudora'd told him she slept on.

"Been thinking, m'dear," he said as they left the room arm in arm, his glossy boots creaking the way his joints felt. "Ought to join forces before the winter sets in. What d'you say, old girl?"

Years ago, as our wedding approached, Jude had spread out a map of Norway on his mother's Regency table and invited me to see where we were going. Together we pondered the threads of road weaving so deftly around blocks of mountain. At one time, he said, his hand sweeping across the wider reaches of Northern Europe, it had belonged to the same land mass. The Highlands of Scotland, for instance, were on a latitude with the southern tip of Norway. Their climate and landscapes were not dissimilar. But during the Ice Age great ruptures occurred, continents separated, islands were born, and even after umpteen millennia, you could see where the jigsaw pieces should have fitted.

Listening to him, I had imagined stormy seas boiling up in the clefts, coastlines fretted by titanic forces of ice, new salients erupting. It never ceased to amaze me how near at hand on an atlas were the places I believed quite inaccessible in life.

"Whew! They're canny, those Norwegians, they knew what they were doing not joining the Market!" Jude exclaimed at an item of BBC News.

"Because they've struck oil?"

"It's one of the largest fields in the world. They'll all be rich as Croesus by the end of the century!"

"Or hanged before noon."

"I know this," he pursued, "come the next election, I'll be voting for the SNP. We've got to husband our own resources. Scotland's played second fiddle too long. Those Sassenachs can keep their thieving fingers out of our pie!"

It was ironic that the very next day a letter arrived from his mother, now Colonel Raven's wife. Relations were still strained and we hadn't learnt of her marriage until a week after it had taken place when we received a call from Heathrow to say she was off to Antibes for her honeymoon. She didn't know how long it would last. Jude recognised her Byzantine hand when he picked up the envelope, though the letters were more sharp and decisive than he remembered.

It was a curt note, uncharacterised by the vague circumlocutions he associated with his parent. As he read it, his face blazed with rage.

"What is it? What's wrong?"

"What's wrong! I'll tell you what's wrong! She's made Raven a wedding gift of her shares!"

"You mean those she was going to transfer to you?"

"Bull's eye!" He flailed the offending document with the back of his hand. "I'm going to get on to Downing right away."

"Your lawyer? But what can he do? A change of heart isn't illegal." It was sometimes expedient to douse Jude's temper by toeing a line not wholly one's own.

"Not illegal! She's sold my birthright. No, not even sold it, she's given it away!"

"She must have been dreadfully unhappy."

"Haven't you any idea what this means?" he challenged. "It means Raven is a major shareholder. Mother will be putty in his hands. Small wonder she's so determined to hold on to the Chairmanship. A stranger, a complete outsider, in control of the Company!"

"He may not want a seat on the Board. He may prefer to let others get on with running the show."

"You can take my word for it, he's had this set up for a while. I knew that *Philistine* had an eye to the main chance! How could she be so blind? How could she do it?"

"You did want your independence..."

"When I think of the way Dad slaved to keep Harmony solvent after the War...!"

Clouds sailed overhead, wisps of white vapour in a blue sky, dispersing, drifting, merging, rediscovering old liaisons. "Angus would have been disappointed," I agreed. "Whatever else could be said of him, he was a family man. He looked after his own."

"A large chunk of those shares is as good as promised to Meredith. Anything could happen to them now. Anything! It's a lunatic thing to do."

"She'll have steered well clear of the Inland Revenue, doing it this way," I said wryly. "There'll be no Capital Transfer Tax to pay."

"Sometimes I wonder if it's all worth it. I mean the political climate's not geared up for survival. Death duties! You can't leave your bootstraps to your children... that is if you manage to achieve the prerequisites of parenthood!"

I hung my head at this malicious shot so that my hair swung down about my face. "Please...please don't." I must talk to him soon. "It isn't the end of the world."


But, daily, as I trod the earth's disintegrating crust, I knew it was a lie. The world was under sentence of death. In the searching light of truth, I saw how 'out of true' its values had become. The vision of New Jerusalem was condemned to everlasting distortion because of the conspiracy of silence about death.

So death, given the offensive, became a foe. He set out to avenge himself, assumed a grimmer visage than need be, deceived by his aptitude for masquerade. He feasted on human fear, abandoning his phantom form and becoming more palpable than life. Death did not suffer a crisis of energy because he consumed ours. Death did not suffer famine or homelessness, did not need to campaign for liberation. Death was having the time of *our* life, laughing behind the backs of those he stalked like a Nemesis, who, in shunning him, were ironically compelled to entertain him at their tables.

It was as though the whole cosmos was afflicted with morbid disease, spreading from tissue to tissue, limb to limb. People walked the streets, pallid and drawn, enervated by hypervigilance and from filling their lungs with pollution. Nowhere was the air really pure. The water they imbibed was not living water; it came from sources poisoned by effluent that had to be filtered and filtered again and still it was tainted and did not refresh the palate. The rivers flowed foul and dark as the Styx, an unwholesome habitation for struggling creatures. Many fish of the rivers wasted and died. Likewise the fish of the sea. For the oil that was spilled on its troubled waters was crude and restored no calm, only clung to the feathers of seabirds, paralysed their wings and bound them to the earth where they perished. They lay strewn on the shores among the cancerous corpses of fish and sea mammals. They were places of great carnage, the borders between water, air and earth: things driven into an alien sphere could not be sustained.

The elements rebelled. There were tornadoes that tore up trees and plucked homes from their foundations. Fire seethed through the earth's fractured shell, spewed molten lava and devastated cities. Elsewhere, tsunamis deluged the landscape, rivers burst their veins and swept through the streets and over hearths, snatching valued possessions. There were gluts and droughts and famines. Scraps of humanity wandered in arid places without food, their flesh shrink-wrapped upon pitiful frames, having nothing to live for but the charity of those more fortunate.

There was no sense to be made of it, none at all.

For the floods could not be harnessed to water the dry plains and what some were deprived of ran to fat on the affluent nations so that their hearts could not bear the weight of their surfeiting and they were starved of life just the same. They knew that tomorrow they would die, so they ate and drank and were merry and plundered the earth until there was no more to be had.

Then they grew pale and threw up their hands in despair. Economy! We must eke out the bit that is left to us. But they had no notion of the principles of economy, had never practised the art. (Could the leopard change his spots or the camel his sinuous spine to pass through the needle's eye?) Economy they equated not with self-investment in a common good, but with grasping whatever they could for as little as possible.

So the deserts encroached year by year and the overwrought soil was harder to till. Folk reaped little reward for the sweat of their brow. But where was the Higher Authority to turn to for guidance in putting their house in order?

*See! God is dead!*

Indeed God was dead, at least dead to the world. God's House was empty, citizens' houses were empty, empty and to let with vacant possession. But the plight of the homeless was mourned up and down. By day they forlornly wandered the streets and at night sought repose in the places of passage, in arcades, under bridges, on stations. There were houses enough and to spare, though not fit for habitation and too costly to repair. We have a new building programme, they were told. When New Jerusalem comes, you shall have palaces. You have only to step on the property ladder.

Then people said to themselves: *What's it all for? Why are we here? Where is the order, the sequence to contain us? To whom can we refer?*

And the doctors dealt out opiates to subdue anxieties and said: *Come back in a fortnight if you do not feel better and can explain in four minutes where it hurts.* The scientists said: *We are on the brink of a discovery, but we need funds.* And the politicians set up commissions on borrowed money to look into matters and said: *We must redistribute the nation's wealth. 'To him that hath shall be given and to him that hath not shall be taken even that he hath'* must be exploited. Our white hope for the poor is the trickle-down effect. And they passed many laws to rectify wrongs. And it was there, on the statute book, that the wrongs had been rectified.

But the honey-tongued psychologists were perhaps the most beguiling of all. They readily acknowledged that humanity was bred from the clay and the mire and that what passed from dust to dust in a continuous revolution could not aspire to be gold. *Nevertheless,* they said, *this is not Life. Life is not full of trauma and injustice. The problem lies buried in infancy when our forebears betrayed us.*

These things sounded rational to ears grown attuned to sophistry. It was comforting to be absolved of all blame. Adam and Eve in the Garden of Eden had been denounced as a myth long ago, but no chink in logic was perceived, only a drain on resources. Folk began to lament the life others had denied them. They nursed their grievances in order to dispel guilt, but only became charged with frustration.

Then some rose up and demanded their rights and the air was oppressive with factions contending for liberation. Terrorists devised weapons and laid them in the path of their brothers. In crowded places they were laid, in streets, aboard planes, beneath cars, in hotel foyers. Men went in search of their lives and wives were widowed at night. The gutters flowed scarlet and children were forbidden to venture outside. A scapegoat was needed and lives were sacrificed to appease the craving for expiation. Many were martyred for the cause, but where was he possessed of so great a love as to lay aside his life for his friend, to find life in losing it? The factions ran to mutually exclusive extremes in pursuit of that strangely inaccessible freedom. *Revolution!* they cried. *More blood must be spilled!* But what had they purchased but debts? Where was the life that was strangled out of existence so that life-swapping, wife-swapping and other desperate diversions were rife? Everywhere humanity was in chains. Hostages were daily held. The prisons were full to overflowing and even a life-sentence shrank to a very few years with good behaviour.

Houses were divided against themselves, the sons from the fathers, the wives from the husbands, upper from lower and sinister from dexter: houses, classes, parliaments, kingdoms, divided and cross-divided against their own allies and partisans. Because in warfare it is necessary to identify with one side or the other, to adopt a totalitarian view and become a pawn in the strategy.

The price of life was death.

Yet mankind subscribed to the Truth it could not swallow and thereby perpetuated the travesty. Kingdoms united in altruistic bonds of self-interest that by economic kinship they might lay claim to quantities of this world's goods and defend themselves from the Enemy in concert.

Meanwhile arms were amassed in dark places underground. It was a matter of pride whose weapons were the most potent, since what could destroy aroused greater awe than the creative capability. It was symbolic indeed, back to front and upside down, that the splitting of what was nuclear and whole, the last resource of integrity, should produce a mine of fresh energy.

Weapons were tested in desolate places to see what they could do. And the whole earth was riven with the dilemma. The aerial structure of the universe was ruptured. Toxic miasmas were released into the ether. Disfigurements and diseases were visited upon the newborn. There was no escape from the cycle of destruction.

But some were beginning to murmur among themselves. *If God is dead, who then has ordained such a fate?* And they looked at one another. They even saw that with a supreme stroke of ego they were rationalising means of mass suicide. How bitter was the revelation – to have to sit down to a banquet of ashes in the throes of starvation. *If God is dead, we are doomed.* They turned and spoke, their voices rising in accusation:

*Where is your panacea, O Doctor?*

*Where your humility, you who advance the frontiers of knowledge?*

*Where is your Monarchy, O Minister of the Crown?*

*Where is the Bridegroom you have espoused, O Church?*

No answer came. Was it possible to weigh anchor in an abyss, or secure belief with a credit card? The predicament produced some deep-seated anxieties. Industries proliferated to maintain the cleanliness mankind had heard tell was the next thing to Godliness. Everything was to be clean and made new, new, new. It was more economical to discard what showed signs of wear than to try to make it good.

Then people began to see their carbon footprints in the sands of time. *We must find a Way Forward*, they said. *We must return to our green innocence, seek Renewable Energy.*

Urgent efforts were made to recycle waste but researchers were hard put to discover the chemistry that would break down indigestible substances and do it cheaply. Unlike the perfect economy of nature which bred life out of decay and achieved its own end with new beginnings.

And while they were there, in their laboratories, scratching their heads over alternative solutions, they stumbled across the first principle of science. They'd learnt it way back from their textbooks, though they didn't know it by heart. *Matter can neither be created nor destroyed.*

O Evolution, Revolution, O Creation turned full circle. What a weight of hope and despair is compounded in that law. What condemnation! What salvation! O Death! O Life!

After a while, I emerged from that winter solstice of the spirit, entombed by dark days, as out of a long, long dream. It was far worse than anything I had yet endured. I had not known what it would cost to see things for what they were worth. I only wanted to sleep, forget. The very daylight impinging on the room each morning brought a flood of dread. Another day. Another battle for survival. Nothing could be taken for granted. The fastening of buttons, the shaking of quilts, loomed insurmountably ahead, an art to be learnt all over again. I was bound by a torpor wound round and round like bandages from which I had neither the strength nor the will to break free. "You must try to pull yourself together," Jude insisted. "Get out more."

Then one morning, I woke to the epiphany of sunrise, watched its arc widen over the rim of the howe and turn the loch to liquid fire. As it was slowly delivered of the earth, I felt I was being reborn. The stone was rolling away. The sun was round and pure as optimism. Independent. Made whole. The tears long imprisoned behind my eyes fell copiously. This was how Lazarus must have felt when he came back to the land of the living.

It was all over then, death, already behind me. And what was it but a nightmare banished at dawn? Or perhaps the draught moaning through a warped lintel against which you might turn up your collar. It wasn't an *event*, yet you saw its effects, felt them. Death was a vicarious thing. It was a term used when others could no longer be seen. Those left behind were the ones who suffered the true death, *those who didn't go on*.

There had been a gale in the night, a faint moaning and soughing gathering force until it screamed round the chimneys and blasted against the windows. The weathered frames juddered, the house shook. Slates slithered off the roof and landed in a broken heap by the door. Jude was on edge. It sounded worse inside. The tremors were amplified. Any minute now, the chimney stack would give way and come crashing through the roof! He imagined wreckage strewn about the garden and tried to recall what insurance we had. He said the premiums were swingeing, but would this be counted as an Act of God? That was the last thing we wanted, he said, to have to fork out for extensive repairs, the price of construction work what it was at present. He suddenly saw all his dreams in ruins, smashed by some arbitrary and unforeseen stroke of fate. Lightning! It couldn't be, could it? Not at this time of year? He jumped out of bed and parted the curtains. Clouds thick as pewter tore across the sky. Pylons swayed down the full length of the glen, cables flailed one another sending out flashes of bleached light. There was a sense of desolation about the little town silhouetted against the darkness. Squares of light pricked the black mass of buildings huddled together, like candles lit in vacant skulls or pumpkin heads on hallowe'en.

He soon realised there was something amiss. There was an openness about the scene. "Hell's bells," he breathed. "It's Fairlie's barn. It's gone! Wiped clean off the face of the earth!"

He'd had a good harvest, had Fairlie, and had set on extra hands to help with the reaping. The bales were packed, right and tight, neat as bricks, up to the roof and anchored down with ropes. "There's few this side o' the glen set up so fine," Fairlie had boasted in the pub. Jude could see the arterial hands, oak-apple brown, scooping up change and gripping the beer mug. "Aye, and that fusionless gowk, Oliphant, can haver about moth and rust! Damn't mon, tisna sense tae chave from dawn tae dusk if tis only tae doon and dee a pauper!"

And there it was, Fairlie's barn a heap of sticks, Fairlie's straw castle besieged, Fairlie's haycocks that stood guard beside it, bowled over, dissolving strand by strand, flying in the wind.

In the houses, the lights went out altogether. The town was plunged into night. One of the great coils of cable sprang off its anchorage and came crashing down. Roofs were ripped off, wind shrieked through the open rafters. Greenhouses were blasted to splinters and seedlings flung into middens and carried afar. The loch lashed and swilled through the dank crevices around its shore, shale rasped and was sucked into the spuming waves.

At the Old Mill, fast off with his wife and bairns, Jamie McBride leapt awake. "The devil! What's that?" Fay screamed and clutched the blankets up to her chest. Icy air flushed through the room and all at once their heads were filled with the hollow roar of water below, the wheel churning like some evil machine that could not be stopped, and everything open to view. The side wall of the house had gone. And Jamie McBride swore a terrible oath and went off into the night, dazed with the shock of it, and wasn't seen again until Tuesday. Clean skite, he went, folk said, and no wonder when you minded that grandfather of his who'd had a touch of the fairlies himself and died polishing his medals with his Glengarry cap on at three in the morning.

They'd never known anything like it in the town. Folk thought it couldn't happen. They fled for cover with neighbours and scrambled about in the dark, coming up against hard and soft clutter in drawers they'd meant to put straight, feeling for candle stubs they'd surely kept for when the power failed. Matches were struck and held up to mildewed cupboards. Old lamps were fetched out filmed with greasy dust, reeking of paraffin and the stringent days of the War. But if the wick wasn't burnt out, there was little or no fuel to be had. Kettles hissed and sang on banked up fires while the gale blew back down the chimney.

But, mercifully, I slept through it all, the sleep of infants.

Dawn came up as mild as a lamb. The sky was transparent. It seemed that praeternatural gold breathed through the pores of the world's jaded fibre. The ramshackle angles, the warped structure of outbuildings, the pale scars of dismembered trees, the spinney which looked as though a god of retribution had smashed a way through, were like a broken language. Words released from the order of sentence and paragraph, from the tyranny of tense and mood. Words burning with new meaning. "And to think," I said, "I didn't know a thing about it."

Jude was anxious to drag me outside to see the damage done, the threadbare roof, the shed door rammed up against a tree and his tools already mottled with rust. Rubbish was lodged in every nook and cranny from the overturned dustbin. "Heaven knows how much this will set us back. The tools alone cost a fortune."

"I can smell spring. There's a definite presage of spring in the air. The way the light falls through the trees is changing."

"Spring! They've snow in the north, blizzards. They've put out avalanche warnings. It's coming this way."

He led me along the overgrown path through the trees and seemed to lose me. Our ways were continuously diverging so that he could derive no comfort now from my optimism. It was of a different order from his own and a threat to him. He no longer had a stake in my life. He said: *"This place is a wilderness. I must get it straight. I must do it soon."*

"We"ll soon have catkins and celandines. There are new buds on the maple, look!"

"It's all right for you. You haven't got our livelihood to worry about."

"Your mother once said that. She said: *It's all right for you, Angel, you're young. Life's on your side.*"

And it was! I seemed to have recovered co-ordination in thought and deed! How laboured my movements had become over the last few months, or was it longer? It was as if what strength I did have seeped away in those pauses between chores so that each became the sole purpose of existence.

Jude didn't see how changes in the light could wreak such a transformation.

"Something's different about you."

But I was at a loss to explain how today was different from all my yesterdays. Perhaps it was the nature of miracles that what appeared to happen in the twinkling of an eye was simply the culmination of a long and secret metamorphosis.

"I knew you'd feel better once you'd had time to get used to it here."

"You look tired," I said. "It is all going as well as you'd hoped? You don't talk about wallpaper these days!"

"You haven't been very approachable," he replied mildly.

"No. No, I'm sorry."

I had been in the grip of a force stronger than myself, cast like flotsam on a tide that was no respecter of persons. It had been as inevitable as night and day, as the whole history of the world running the gamut of its emotions in a sequence of action and reaction.

"We're having a bit of cash flow trouble," Jude admitted.

"It seems to be everybody's problem at the moment."

"I'm not my own man any more," he complained. "An MD with no shares to speak of!"

"Are *they* for a change of policy, then?"

"No, not yet."

"You sound doubtful."

"I can see it coming."

I wanted to reassure him and say that things weren't so bad. But I could offer no spurious comfort.

But we aren't trapped for ever, I wanted to say. We don't have to go round on the same old circuit, seeing the same old signs again and again. The years of Grace are a turning point in Time.


I hadn't realised until my head touched the pillow that I was spent. My pulse hammered in my very teeth so that they banged together. But sooner than usual, the disjointed pain in my chest faded. Something gave, like a sluice-gate bursting open, and the blood gushed freely through my veins.

My mind floated. I began to focus on a vivid subliminal landscape suspended in perfect consciousness between sleep and wakefulness, a hypnogogic sphere which did not enlist emotion or response or cause loss of that state we call 'reality'. It was like a film, with its own immanent life-force, and entirely unlike the duller picture conjured up at will in the mind's eye.

A chasm emerged, two crude promontories cloven to the foundations, parting little by little to reveal white mists curling out of a deep blue infinity. But in the space, a great shadow appeared in the shape of a Cross, embedding its spars into the rock as if to weld them together, as if to make a bridge. The shadow was emblazoned with light like a sun-in-splendour, inenarrable light of glassy gold. And in the Cross, at this the Crux of the Paradox, the farthest extremes were eternally met so that nothing but nothing should ultimately be given over to chaos. In this vicarious Death on behalf of mankind, the tide of consequences was stemmed and the price of Life paid, so that human beings might look *forward* to the future and *profit* from their handiwork.

A pall of cloud began to steal the vision and hide the outlines of the chasm. This is the only way I can describe the spirit and sense of it:

*After the holocaust, smouldering odours lingered over the irradiated Earth. The ground was covered with dry thistle. Flock and cattle had died in the fields, their flesh putrefying in the heat of the day and their bones bleached to chalk. Trees withered, their foliage hanging in strings. They groped out of the soil like charred hands. Birds had plummeted from the sky in vast numbers, but the blasphemous stink of scorched feathers did not revive the senses of humanity.*

*People pondered on the illusions they had once held dear. They were starved of rest, scratching the soil for a handful of grain that slipped through their fingers in a moment's distraction. The fabric of dwellings crumbled away as dust. Fountains had ceased, rivers and lakes had evaporated. The sun was a furnace and people cried out for refuge, for a slaking shade and the water of Life. Their flesh had desiccated and the ravages of a lifetime were wrought in days and a lifespan's wisdom found no application. Much was expended for a diminishing return, for such were the laws of inflation and such was the structure they had committed themselves to. The light was brighter than a desert noon, searing the ball of the eye. In the crook of their elbow men buried their heads and elected to keep the darkness of their souls.*

*And this was the day they had craved, when all clouds should be gone from the sky.*

*There were many works of devastation, a breaking down as revolutionaries have long sought with counterfeit coin. But when scourges multiplied, when stars shot out of their courses and the seasons fell out of turn and the rains were subdued, when yardsticks were altered and a universal mode of thought generated its own confusion, we were not to fear. A change was coming to pass. Beneath the parched ground was the sound of many waters. Now the Earth groaned like a woman in travail, broken apart by the pangs of a new creation.*

*For three elements were polluted and set at war with one another; earth, air and water. But the fourth was sacred; it could not be destroyed. And with this element, Creation would be purified, the gold and the dross running together for aeons would be separated. Nothing would stand in the fire but what was True, until all that glistered should at last be Gold.*

*The old order would dissolve into ashes and there would be a New Heaven and a New Earth.*

# Evening

*The Angel that presided o'er my birth*
*Said, "Little creature formed of joy and mirth,*
*Go, love, without the help of anything on earth.*

# Evening

My easel stood idle, my colours tubed.

I began to consider what might be achieved with my paintbrush. Something, surely. Had I lost the compulsion? Perhaps I should seek a new medium. Perhaps I was *living* the picture and no longer needed to paint, at least not for the same reasons.

Spring came. There were mild days and bleak. Snowdrops arrived silent as apparitions among last year's leaves and the criss-crossed wood snapped off in the gale. Below the window, in the patch of ground I'd cleared, green shoots poked through in orderly array. And suddenly, I saw how it would be, daffodils, tulips, flame-centred narcissi standing sentinel around my bit of earth, brightly blooming after the dead tints of winter, the pain of the sowing long forgotten.

"The trouble is," Jude said, "you've only to have one bad frost at this time of year and they're finished."

I was about to reply that spring plants were generally hardy. They could take swift changes of temperature, but I stopped short. He was right. Plans could be nipped in the bud.

For a full fortnight the technicians had worked on the telephone lines, shinning up poles, referring to diagrams, trying this connection and that. Many folk in the glen were experiencing difficulty getting through to the outside world.

"Wouldn't you think," Jude slammed down the receiver after trying to contact John Meredith seven times, "that in these days of advanced technology it could have been put right long before now?"

He was easily deflated of late. The joy had gone out of living and not even my apparent recovery really affected him. There was no tantalising prospect ahead, just day after dreary day of coping with the practical problems of existence which seemed engaged in a war of attrition against him. He became obsessed with his mother's perfidy.

One evening, he raced home from the office and took me by surprise, colliding with me on the doorstep, I going out to pick herbs, he coming in. "Come quickly! There's a beautiful sunset! Come and see!"

"But I can see it from the window!"

"No, you can't. Not to advantage."

He snatched my sheepskin from its hook and placed it around my shoulders, leading me off to the car, its engine still running. We drove to a high point over moorland strewn with dead rabbits and a slain lamb by the wayside. With so little traffic the animals roamed without caution. The sight of their mangled bodies was distressing, the pink entrails ground into their fur, the cruel alizarin stains. But Jude, bent on getting there before the sun vanished, put his foot down and saw nothing. We reached a spot marked by a cairn, said by some to be a place of burial, by others to indicate the way.

The sky was breathtaking. Molten gold poured down between the mountain ridges, lending them the incorporeal appearance of smoke-coloured glass. A breeze was constantly changing pitch as though it played over the mouthpiece of a harmonica. Eternity was within touching distance.

"Trust me," Jude said. "Trust me as you used to do. Listen, I've been thinking..."

"About what?"

"Plans for the future. *Diversification*."

I sighed. All at once I could barely support my own weight. Another pinnacle to view the kingdoms of the world!

We stood in silence.

"We'd better go back," he said at length, turning away.

I felt his defeat, that he had failed to touch me, but I could not help him. Another influence pervaded the glen, inspired the wispy trees. New plumes, pale green, were unfurling above the dead bracken. In the east, the sky was a voluminous blue, the ring of a transparent moon rising. For a while, the sun and the moon occupied one firmament, ascending and descending their predestined trajectories.

Driving back, I began to be aware of an oddness in Jude's bearing which had escaped me on the way there. An unfamiliar fragrance hung about the car. I leaned back and kicked off the loafers from my hard-pinched feet which were usually swollen by this time of day. My heel came into contact with a foreign object, hard and round. A stone? I bent down and held it up to the dwindling light.

"What's that you've found?" Jude asked. Did I fancy a note of alarm?

"A pendant."

"A pendant?"

"But not on a chain."

A stone. A small cabochon turquoise set in a halo of diamond chips, or even spinels, or paste, it was hard to tell."

"It must be Marnie's. I think she has something of the kind."

"Marnie?"

"Marilyn, my new PA." There was a false note in his voice, not of alarm, of defensiveness.

"Of course." I had met Marilyn once. A winsome Scot with laughing green eyes that took the gravity out of the situation. There was a ripple of humour in everything. Marilyn.

"She went to the bank today. I let her borrow the car."

I imagined him dangling the keys of his precious Mercedes under the girl's nose, dropping them into the palm of her hand. *Bring it back in one piece,* he'd say. *I'm living on credit as it is.*

"She clearly has her feet under the dashboard!"

"Damn! I'm low on petrol. Better drop in at the garage before they close. "Got an early start in the morning."

We pulled up in the neon glare of the forecourt. "You'd better take this," I said unsteadily. "Let her have it back tomorrow."

Jude took the pendant and without a word dropped it into his top pocket where it nestled with a wad of die-stamped calling cards. The metre ran up like laddered hose.

I thought of them, Jude and Marilyn together, she with her Gaelic lilt and he with his disengaged manhood, and what was like grit under the shell was that *I* had left room for the Interloper in the spot were the tear of pearl should have formed.

My failure to fly into a jealous passion irked him to the point of informing me that, yes, he was sleeping with her and if I was any sort of wife it would never have happened.

I simply did not have the energy to contest it. Or even to care about the treason itself. The affairs of the flesh lagged way behind. The human body had begun to look like an alien structure, its functions quite bizarre, with the blood swilling around its plumbing, its odd reflexes, and its perpetual drive to host colonies of elementary life forms. I had no idea what I would have preferred in its place, but I was no longer at home with it.

"It's only you I want," Jude said pathetically.

"It wasn't when you had me."

The wind stirred and rushed among the young leaves outside. And it was the same wind, laced with promise, that had sighed through the glen earlier that evening. The night air came in, fernlike and green. The sun was burnt out now, the last traces of pink gone cold.

The moon slowly silvered and came into its own.


The letter read:

*Dear Mrs Brightman,*

*I tried to ring you today, but couldn't get through. This is just to let you know that the books you ordered are now in stock and await collection.*

*Yours sincerely,*
*Adam Goodfellow.*

Nothing special in that, but why should there be? I folded it up and then opened it again. A strange warmth rose off the dead, metallic type. And I remembered the newly coined moon, how the circle had filled up with silver, and the skirl of the wind on the brae. This land was mine, I its. I was slowly imparting myself to this earth so that its rhythms, its very exhalations were my own. And I recalled something else, a half-revived impression of a presence passing and repassing through my dreams whom I recognised and I didn't. A whiff of tobacco came up from the page.

So I put on my coat and set off for the town, hearing my tread scuff over the pavement, as though I looked in upon Angel. Speedwell sprang, sapphire-blue, out of the ditches.

Soon I came to the bookstore and, lifting the latch, went in. A bell rang somewhere in the depths of the premises. It was dim and bright together in there, the kind of dimness that lends dimension to colour. The bullioned panes made rainbow shadows on the dust-jackets of the window display. It smelled of old leather and tobacco, the sweet decadence of gilt-edged pages stuck fast with mildewed age. It was like stepping into another world, shutting out the rush and boom of the traffic on its way to the next place.

The sound of soft shoes padding down a flight of stairs changed pitch. I turned, and all at once he materialised, silent as a gift, bending his head to get through the small panelled door and unfolding his long limbs: Adam Goodfellow, New and Antiquarian Books. For a split second, I was stunned. The dream atmosphere brushed against me, the figure I knew and didn't know! I vaguely supposed that my shock had communicated itself to him, for a look of startled disbelief arrested him mid-motion.

It was on the tip of my tongue to say: *Don't I know you? Haven't we met somewhere before?* But it was unlikely. Besides, he was giving nothing away, not then.

"I'm Angel Brightman," I ventured. "You've some books for me, I believe."

A smile of such artless pleasure and sympathy and astonishment commingled broke over his features. I was taken aback by it, for his was a grave face. The eyes harboured a look of mellowed regret, though his temples were scored by humour. I had a prickly feeling that he was laughing at me, that he had surprised some awful caricature I had never suspected. But when I looked into the eyes that were grey and should have been a dark velvet brown, I acquitted him. There was not an ounce of derision in him. He was laughing *with* me. We were on the same side!

He produced from under the counter a pile of five or six books. "I'll wrap them for you," he said, and dived through the door into the back of the shop, returning with brown paper labelled from previous use and some squares of old cardboard cut down to size. He'd an arrangement with the wine merchant next door and the grocer over the road. With smooth, economical movements he wrapped the books, laying the spines neatly together. He drew up the ends of the paper to meet in a fleet fold and you wondered that he should have contrived it so well, he scarcely touched anything, yet so unhurried he seemed. Slender his hands were, the nails beautifully pared, the knob of the wrist well-formed but delicate. You imagined it bent round the strings of a violin, or the fingers treading the perforations of a flute so that music poured out like liquid. Lithe he was, neither young nor yet middle-aged exactly, bursting with a quiet exuberance, and I remembered the 'lithe' that meant 'shelter' in Scotland.

I could see that the back rooms were crammed with his scavengings, all labelled and organised so that particular copies might be easily located: gems found under the dust in attics after the owner's demise, oddments from precious collections taken apart under the auctioneer's hammer. It was deeply saddening, he later told me, what death and inflation could do to years of patience and taste in the building of a library. At least, he said, it made these treasures accessible. His entire stock was born of the tension between the desire to handle a certain rare volume and the wisdom of purchasing several dozen with a wider appeal. He seldom bought what he really disliked.

My eyes flashed over the compact rows and their colours seemed to spring to life. Each volume was a door into a charmed world. The topography, the history, the poetry and mystery, all were aspects of his personality.

There was something about him that made me feel cornered, but not in any unpleasant way. Whether it was good or not, I *assented* to it.

"I was interested in your choice of books," he remarked. His voice was gentle, mellifluent, with a wealth of inflexion. "You aroused my curiosity."

"Oh?" I turned towards him.

"I don't often get asked for these, certainly not all at once. I was staggered when my assistant showed me your list."

"Some books I'll beg, steal or borrow, some I prefer to buy!"

"These are only for lovers of fine art," he said, as though welcoming me to some esoteric sect. "Chagall, the Novecento Movement, Ruskin, the Norwich School…"

"There are so many ways of approaching a landscape…"

"As an artist, I take it?"

"An uninspired one mostly," I laughed. "I've been unwell for a while but it's given me time to *think*."

"And recharge the batteries. Of crucial importance."

"Now I'm a lot better, I have a crazy urge to take up the brush again. I want to tackle landscape in a new and more truthful way. I want to lose the impression that I'm seeing it *through glass*."

"It's a good idea to break new ground sometimes," he agreed in a manner that was both absorbed and distant at once, weighing his words and yet not consciously doing so. You felt he was drawing on experience rather than maintaining a general principle. Even such a simple exchange cost him something, yet it was delivered with the natural ease of one far from bankruptcy. He didn't make you feel obliged to respond. Beneath the kindness and humour, I surprised a sheer hunger for affection. But he was no beggar, he would pick and choose, walking a tightrope into his relations with others. Someone has hurt you, I thought. You don't smart any more, but you cannot forget. Whoever she was, she would have been beautiful, with a voice more demanding than yours and a name like Elizabeth, or Elspeth or Evangeline. I glanced at his hands, knowing the tentative touch of them, tentative but sure, the unstinting devotion with which they would cherish the object, and how in the end it would slip away fleet and bright as the quicksilver pain deep within me. It was haunting, that clandestine knowledge of love in his eyes that were grey and should have been brown.

He handed over the package, strung and securely knotted. The books were protected with card that told of distilled spirits and honey 10p off the recommended price. "There! Will that be all right? Can you manage?"

I thanked him and said it would be fine, though no proper sound came out. Unclasping my purse, I heard the street door open behind me. The world gatecrashed the shop with the strident blast of a horn and the hollow chatter of milk bottles gliding past on a float. The bell rang in a beady jet of alarm. I remembered the empty house I must return to and Jude prowling round like a caged animal in the small hours in search of alcohol. I hated waking to the stale, astringent smell in the morning, and perhaps it was because I rebelled so strongly against the incursion that whoever it was turned tail and went off down the street on some other errand.

Adam Goodfellow raised his brows and looked mildly affronted. I wanted to laugh. I gave him my debit card which had nearly expired. On the spur of the moment, I panicked, wanting to draw back from the transaction, as though I had squandered my life savings on something frivolous. Revulsion against some notion too perfect to contemplate swept through me and I couldn't bear the thought of the constant warring of the will with Jude. I was worn out with it all. The force of the emotion shook me.

"Do let me know if there's anything else I can find for you," Adam offered. "I've had quite a lot of luck tracing some pretty old editions. It's very rewarding to find something rare."

Yes, I said in a whisper, I'd do that. The Celtic knot carving on the cornice began to pass from left to right, gathering speed. I took a deep breath.

"Is anything wrong?"

"I...it will pass."

"Look, why don't you come inside and sit down for a few minutes. I was just about to make a pot of tea as a matter of fact."

Before I could decline, as I was about to do, not wishing to put him to trouble, he said: *Do come* in a way which made me feel I should be giving as well as accepting. I felt profoundly relieved.

He led me into the parlour and indicated a buttoned armchair the colour of rain-drenched moss, hastening to remove a stack of dusty books from the seat. I sank into it gratefully. At least the ground would not be cut from under my feet now. "It is kind of you," I said.

"Not at all," he replied with that potent mixture of intimacy and formality which had pervaded his letter. "You could have a drop of brandy if you'd rather."

"No, thank you... I don't know what to say."

"Say nothing... It isn't always necessary."

I was soothed by his presence and by this room as I had never been soothed in my life. It was tranquil, in shades of jade and onyx green. The curtains fell in soft easy folds. I liked its masculine textures of leather and corn-coloured canework creaking as it relaxed in the atmosphere: the dense surfaces and the openwork freely inviting the eye. It was neither ascetic nor lavish. In fact the amount of furniture was inclined to be spare, but what there was was of good quality and well-used. A striking blend of Victorian and new falling together into an arrangement you recognised but would not have dreamed of yourself. The light in the room was sharp and clear. Outside a larch swayed gently against the sky, arousing the poignant feeling that larches always did, I couldn't tell you why. Perhaps it was some shred of inherited memory or an adumbration of the present. I thought how unlikely it was to be here with this stranger, faint but not having to hide it, who did not pester me for responses. A stranger who wasn't a stranger at all. When I looked into his face, I knew him through and through, knew him, loved him, and the only place I wanted to be in the world was there in his arms.

A tangle of honeysuckle overhung the window. In a month or two its fragrance would come floating in across the desk where he worked, a mountain of books on ancient cultures ranged around him. He was writing a piece for a periodical at the moment, he explained, archaeology and geology were his subjects. I told him I'd been to Corinth. Had he seen it? Yes, he said, the old city stranded so far from the new. It haunted him that such a civilisation could be lost and forgotten and the lessons have to be learnt all over again.

"It's something you have to *see*," I agreed. "You can't explain it. You could go there time and again and listen to numerous guides and still not fully grasp that."

He produced a small bamboo table and placed it between my chair and the chesterfield. Then he poured tea and gave me a cup, pushing the sugar basin warily towards me, a trifle unsure of his luck. It was as if I had long set my heart on a gift it was his to bestow and he was watching me unwrap it.

"I wasn't expecting a visitor," he said, half-apologising for the state of the room.

I sipped tea. It ran down hot and welcome inside, such thin innocuous stuff to be doing so much good. "An invasion," I smiled, "of your workspace."

"No invasion. Your feet are so small. Ballerina's feet."

He settled back on the chesterfield, silent for a moment, but his eyes lived a life of their own, smouldering and alert. When he did move, he would silently spring into action and his limbs would seem to compose themselves in slow motion around their objective. I had a vague but gnawing impression of having observed a similar trait in others, I couldn't recall who or where, as though I had long been striving towards this consummation. I said to myself: *you lope and I don't like interlopers*, but was immediately smitten with remorse and when he bent his head to drink tea, I was stung with a sadness so acute I was never to think of it afterwards without an onrush of tears.

It was safe there, a haven, where life was absorbed between the pages of books and the minutiae of daily existence.

"Have you lived long in the town?" he asked.

"We came last autumn. From Leicestershire."

"They're marvellous people, the Scots, whatever those Sassenachs tell you. You'll like it this side of the border."

"You've been here some time?"

"About seven years now. I certainly don't hanker to return to London. We lived in Montmartre for a while."

I was studying the painting above the mantelpiece, searching it. There was a companion piece on the wall behind him. "Isn't it strange how pictures lend atmosphere to a whole space?"

"I take them for granted, I suppose."

"They remind me of…Tissot, I think." They were street scenes with a Parisian 1890s air, lime-tinted trees and baroque architecture. In one a man and a woman were walking side by side, caught in a shower of rain. He was tall and inclined toward her, sheltering her under an umbrella. She was looking down at the pavement, watching the progress of her own feet. You couldn't see her expression but everything about her emanated beauty. She was wearing a long dress of some pink diaphanous material, organdy perhaps, which looked luminous against the grey street. The signature was so faintly etched into the paint that it was only legible upon close scrutiny.

"I knew the artist...once upon a time." Adam mused, not without a speck of rancour. "Will you have more tea?"

I thanked him and shook my head. "I must go." I wanted to stay there for ever, to make things *come right*.

He got up to open the door. "Will you be all right now? I could close the shop for while and drive you home."

"I wouldn't dream of it. I'll be fine...honestly." He followed me out of the parlour and overtook me to open the outer door. Our reflections merged on the street-shadowed glass as I said goodbye.


Adam did not say goodbye. He watched Angel walk up the street and disappear, carrying the parcel under her arm. She wasn't using the string loops he had made for her. He turned back into the shop, overcome by a feeling of futility. Cologne lingered on the air, warm and profound and green. Life was suddenly empty and purposeless. When he slid the red frame over the day on the calendar that morning, he hadn't expected it to matter.

Returning to his ancient Remington, he scanned the two or three lines he'd typed at the top of the sheet just before the shop bell rang and she entered his life. Pulling it from the carriage, he screwed it up and dropped it into the waste basket, wondering how he could have written phrases so banal. He turned up a clean sheet and tried to pick up the threads of his exposition, but her face loomed out of the vacant page, the eyes with an ingenious light in them which took him into their ken. There was something about her you could not put your finger on. A *disembodied* aura. Despite that, in her company he had felt light-headed and elated, a sharer in a secret joke.

He hoped that next time she came it would not be a day when he was out and Esther was minding the shop.

That she would come back, he had no reason to doubt.

The bell shrilled again, piercing the silence, and made him start. It was an aging schoolteacher with silver-grained hair requesting a copy of *Paradise Lost*.


So that was my meeting with the bookseller of Glenfinnie. My shoes took me back through a town that wasn't Glenfinnie at all, another place altogether viewed that way on and lost in an otherworld air. There had been a shower which surprised me. Droplets spangled the awnings over some of the shops.

The air was laden with the tang of fir woods and awakening heather. I dragged my leaden feet up the hill, brushing the newly-minted dandelions along the verges. The parcel grew heavy beyond reason and impeded every step. I stopped for breath and looked back over the town, over the wet roofs and waxing gardens, and nowhere but nowhere did the larches aspire strong and gentle as they did in the heart of Glenfinnie.

The house offered no welcome. It was silent and cold. The central heating had been turned down in order to save on the worst quarter's bill. Last time the meter was read, Jude had whistled. He insisted there was something wrong with the system, but no fault could be found upon investigation.

I debated whether to light a fire. I was supposed to be guarding against chills. There were no logs in the hearth. I'd have to go out to the stable and fetch some. I stared at the gaping grate and then the bolt struck me, the anguish of loss. I had supposed I was immune to such ineffable pain, it was all finished for me. Panting, I dropped into a chair. The clock tolled melodiously. The eleventh hour. Adam, I said in a bereft whisper. *Adam!*

It was Jude who rescued me from that black infinitude. The swish and crunch of tyres pulling up sharp on the gravel took me by surprise. The car door slammed and he stormed in, his face dark as thunder.

"Jude?" He made straightaway for the decanter and slopped a liberal quantity of Scotch into a glass.

"I've had one hell of a row with Meredith," he announced. "He wants to quit."

"Oh?"

"Says there's no future for him at Harmony. We're not living up to his expectations."

"He has his own life to make, I suppose," I said with weary detachment, mentally replacing the stopper he had left off.

"But he was all for expansion!"

"He *has* been let down over the question of shares."

"That could have been organised, given time. Or concessions in lieu. This is no time to abandon ship."

"When it's sinking?"

"We've laid ourselves out and are in a vulnerable position at the moment. No one could foresee that we'd be having to chase accounts left, right and centre in order to pay our bills. Or that we'd have problems keeping labour. That's the drawback with being on an industrial estate; workers play off one firm against another all the time. We can't meet our delivery dates." He took a large gulp and turned his back upon me to stare out of the window. "Swine!"

I closed my eyes and took a deep breath. A passionate resentment welled up inside that he should be here occupying so much space, blocking out the light. I did not want him encroaching upon my grief. "Haven't you got work to do?"

"Yes, of course I've got work to do," he snapped. "I wanted to get away for a while and think."

Had he come to bolster his confidence with my support of the line he had taken? "I wish you hadn't quarrelled with your mother."

He threw me a laser glance, uncertain how to take this. "Meredith's a fool. He's not given the thing a chance to work. In a year or two, we'll be sailing with the wind. And, by then, I'll be in a position to buy Raven out with any luck. It's only a question of time!"

Ah time, I wanted to say. The Enemy is never on our side.

Later, after Jude had gone and the heavens were clear of rain, I realised the exorcism I had performed in denying him the consolation he sought. It was not merely an exorcism of his influence, but of my own pain, so that when I recaptured the world of Adam Goodfellow, I no longer suffered that agony of loss. I couldn't picture his face, not for days, but felt a closeness so acute it might have been telepathic. The incense of his personality was burning all around me and I cherished it and wore it like an amulet, persuaded that nothing and no one could take it away.

But I mustn't dwell on him. Adam. I was dazed by all the love encapsulated in that syllable. No previous experience had prepared me for such an avalanche of emotion. With Jude, I had fallen in love *backwards*. We had met on a youth holiday among the glittering Alps. He had picked wild roses and gentians for me (illegally, as was his wont!) at Kleine Scheidegg station halfway up the Jungfrau. I was irritated by his arrogance, by the way he took life and moulded it to his own design. He pursued me, I strongly discouraged him, he wrote, he came rapping on the door of the flat I shared with two other girls, late one night, saying he was passing through the town, could we put him up? The bath would do if there was nowhere else. It was pouring with rain, he was soaked and bedraggled and swore he was saving up for a mac. So I gave in, for what woman is proof against such ardour? Soon I was swept along with him and, sweet it was, I discovered, after the emotional co-operatives of St Mary's Home and the unnerving expanses of the big, wide world, to have someone of my own to defer to. His very arrogance was what I came to rely upon and what, in the end, betrayed me.

129

I vowed I would never go to the bookshop again. I would not see Adam. I would ring him and tell him I didn't need the book he had left out of the parcel. For when I unwrapped my purchases, I found that one title was missing. He hadn't charged me for it, but it was plainly listed on the invoice he had receipted. It was easy to guess what had happened. When he was picking up the pile from under the counter, he failed to grasp the lowest book. In a flash of intuition, I saw those precise movements and it dawned on me that a person with instincts as thrifty as his might well exploit a slip of this kind on the spur of the moment. Did he mean me to go back? I dismissed the idea as absurd. But why had he gone to the trouble of deducting it from the bill? I couldn't get it out of my mind, that slim volume lying there in the shadows waiting for me to claim it.

The matter was left to ride for the rest of the week and over the week-end. By Tuesday morning, however, I had run out of money and a visit to the bank was clearly indicated. The window-cleaner might call, or a charity envelope be pushed through the box, I reasoned with all the urgency of one threatened with litigation for an unpaid bill.

Adam was poring over an ordnance map when I stepped into the shop. He looked up with an expression of questioning surprise, a slight gleam in his eye. "I thought you weren't coming," he said lightly. A contrite grin spread over his features.

It was true, then. *It was true.* Well, of course it was, I thought in a sudden access of arguable logic. How could it not be? Whether to laugh or to scold?

"I wondered if I'd made a mistake. I mean, I wasn't sure whether the book would be needed after all."

"You had your doubts, then?" He brought out the book and placed it on the counter, a slim edition, the print smaller than average.

"I couldn't let you down. You mightn't have been able to sell it to anyone else."

He took my debit card uncertainly. "I'd have missed you if you'd come half an hour later. Esther's holding the fort this afternoon. I'm going to view a sale. You could come with me if you've nothing better to do."

"To a book sale?"

"Why not? You'd be interested."

"Well, I..." I turned aside. Life had to be met through ever narrowing apertures these days. The chores had to be staggered, the shopping on Tuesday and the ironing Wednesday, if exhaustion were not to swamp me. An outing so imminent was too overwhelming to be entertained. I might be stranded with nowhere to rest. "Is it far? I have to get back, you see."

"Kintully Castle. It's twenty miles or so. That isn't far. I know a nice teashop we could go to, scones and damson jam and lashings of cream. You're not on a diet, are you?"

He knew he had won, knew it from the first. The possibility of not winning was no more than a courtesy.

"I must leave a message for Jude. He won't expect me to be out, at least not for long. Oh, an excursion! It's a long time since I went on one of those!"

Inside twenty minutes, we were away, purring along arcades of delicate green injected with sunlight. You had missed the coming of spring yet again, though you swore that this year the miracle would not escape you. All you noticed were the softly crowding lanes, the altered chiaroscuro.

We turned on to a bumpy track and followed a Landrover bouncing and crackling under a row of pines. There between the blending greens, we espied patches of oyster-coloured granite.

"That must be the castle," I said.

"East of the Sun and West of the Moon!"

Conical turrets emerged between the trees. "Who'd suspect that was there so close to the beaten track?"

"Solid enough to deter any marauding Sassenach," Adam said, betraying the pleasure of those who give gifts.

"Have you been before?"

Adam shook his head. "I knew it was here. They tell of it back in Glenfinnie. But I haven't had occasion, until now."

"Is it being sold up, then?"

"Sadly, the Laird of Dunross can no longer afford to maintain it. A sign of the times, I'm afraid."

"But what will become of it?"

"I suppose if no Arab sheikh comes along, it will be turned into a school or some kind of admin. centre." Obeying the chalked signs, Adam drove into a cobbled yard and slid into a space between the antique dealers' estate cars. "At this stage, I always feel like one of the vultures gathering over carrion."

"But couldn't it have been taken over by some heritage body? The National Trust, for instance, have to keep everything as it is. It's *inalienable*."

He seemed half-amused and half-perturbed by my dismay. "I'd like to tell you that the castle will be spared from Arabs and local councils and any other contenders for the kingdom, but who can make that sort of promise?"

My gaze fell and I saw that my hand was resting in his. He had stolen a march on me when my mind was elsewhere. "Where did you come from, so late in the day?" I said in a strained whisper.

"Now why was I thinking those precise words?"


"One thing that is surprising," Adam remarked as we drove back over the moors after tea, "at least many people find it so when they begin to investigate the geology of Scotland..."

"What?"

"That it's a land rich in gold."

I smiled through my weariness. The words had a familiar ring! "I've heard tell of ghillies who lay sheepskins in streambeds and wake up rich men!"

"The problem is that the cost of extraction is uncommercial." He pulled up on the brow of a hill. "Come with me, I'll show you something."

He took my hand, quite naturally, as though he were leading a child, strong and bent on a purpose I had no inkling of. Oh, where was he taking me over earth scorched last summer where the crofters had burned off the heather? On some fool's errand? On a wild goose chase? There were no landmarks in sight. Not a tumbled cairn to be seen. But then, I heard a soft rushing sound as of distant harmony. "I can hear water, can't I?"

The sound rang truer and the ground began to vibrate gently underfoot. And there it was! It poured out at our feet, spindrift flying over the rocks. "It's lovely, isn't it?" I cried, mesmerised by the sparkle and the ephemeral patterns chased by the flow. Our voices were snatched up into the music's curvature and carried away down the glen.

"It is lovely," Adam agreed, "but it isn't what we came to see." He pointed to a little basin where the water pooled and slid in fine strands over the brim. He plunged in his hand and picked out a pebble, smooth as a coin, and dashed it against a rock so that it broke in two. Inside he showed me tiny granules of glinting metal, a faint mustard-coloured sheen as of light diffused though a film of dust.

"Fool's gold?"

"No, the real McCoy!"

In astonishment I gazed down into the water and it seemed that my eye annexed patch upon patch of the same metallic lustre shimmering through the diffracted light there. "But there's so much of it!"

"The last vestiges of a Golden Age."

"Pity about the dross!"

"It will come again. We shall reach the bright point in the cycle and the wheel will stop for ever. What has been so dearly proved will never be lost again. By going forward, we shall find our way back. We must *work...*"

"But the labour...the sheer patience," I foundered. Words failed at so daunting a prospect. But even as I spoke, I saw again running in the rock a dim nexus of arteries, pollen-gold with the germination of a new order.

"Anodyne toil," Adam said. "Stones made bread. It is a way and a means, but no longer an end. *I gave you a land where you never toiled, you live in towns you never built; you eat now from vineyards and olive groves you never planted.*"

He spoke soothingly, as he might to a bewildered child. His voice was vibrant and full of lustre, a voice which knew its own range and its keynote and made full use of them. He was so unlike Jude, eager for despatch at all costs and never mind the friction it caused.

"Why did you show me?"

"Because you needed reminding...and so did I."

Thin rays were coming through verdigris clouds, fanning out on the hillside. Tears slid helplessly down my cheeks. Reaching out, he drew me close, closer than I had been to anyone in my life, and let me drown in the comfort I had wanted and willed and cried out for. It was sweet to know the bedrock of another will. "What is it about you?" he murmured over and over. "You're so strong in some ways, so defenceless in others. ...I love you."

The sweetness soon hardened into guilt. All my craving for someone to lean on, a need so cogent it could not fail to invoke a response, was being charged to Adam's account. It was he who was making ends meet for me. "Don't...don't love me too much."

"It's too late for that," he said. I tried to think coherently but couldn't, only let out a halting sigh. What arrogance it had been to protect Jude! I had distrusted the promise of Grace enough for every need. Only when I could bring myself to say what I had to say would I find absolution and the strength to help him cope. The world had seemed too frail a place to support the truth. But this was the fire in which it would be refined and proved and annealed. These were the very acts to usher in a New Heaven and a New Earth.

"And now I must take you back," Adam said. "Come and see me tomorrow or the next day, if you can. Come through the garden by the lane at the back. Come straight in. I'll leave the door on the latch."

He bent down to pick a lone flower which he gave to me, grinning with boyish delight. "A wild pansy. An early one."

I stroked its velvety face. "Heartsease," I said. "How clever of you to spot it."


Often since he had known Angel, Adam was taken unawares by pangs of nostalgia springing from nowhere. Now, the dank taste of evening clung to his palate and there came to his mind a vision of Elizabeth in the latter days of her pregnancy when she had been in a position of weakness and he of strength, able to fetch and carry for her, to take her upon his arm. Strange to remember how he had spread his hands upon her distended belly and known the thrust of that life which burgeoned between them, wondering at its purpose in the scheme of things and where it had been before the moment of conception. She said that somewhere in infinity a soul was crying out to be given access to life, but he had not seen it in those terms. It had been gratuitous, a gift. Dear fool, she'd said tenderly, patting his cheek. But he had never lost that pure sense of wonder. As time passed, it became informed with a gentle wisdom. Indeed it had been his salvation, forestalling cynicism where caution would serve.

Those were perfect months, fecund months. She had wanted him very much then, the shadow and the substance of him. They had been happily absorbed in their own enchanted world. But perhaps it was a sin to be so prodigally in love. There was no place for it in the wider context and the narrow one soon became congested with all they wanted to express. One evening, at a charity ball, he made some playful remark but failed to catch her eye. She smiled without humour and turned on a flash of shot taffeta to address an unknown young man, a sculptor, it transpired. Adam might have ceased to exist. The dress was new, only bought that week. He had given her an open cheque for her birthday.

He withdrew from the dance floor into that realm of restive movement upon its periphery. He didn't care for dancing, but for her he would do it and could do it well. The faces around him were mask-like and grotesque in the half-light. Illusions of gems shone from the shadows. He took out his pipe as he often did in moments of retreat, but there was nothing pleasant in his speculations now. Through a shifting blue-grey veil he watched the two of them, seeing them clearly, not seeing them at all. Peals of silvery laughter broke from their eclipsing figures, laughter in a key he didn't recognise. Ah Beth! He had chosen to call her that with its flavour of sweetness and patience. She was capricious at times: it was one of her charms, but he had not understood the force of his own steadying influence upon her. Was she, after all, a mere chameleon borrowing colour from her surroundings? Was that what he had wanted, a projection of himself? Why had such a trivial incident violated his whole conception of her? He smarted, not because she had snubbed him, but because he did not really know her.

When, later, he claimed her and trod the measures of the dance, he knew that he had lost her. She could not follow him. He strove to atone for the casualties of her step and thought of the child at home asleep in his cot. Later still, in bed, he turned to her and tried to make it right, but it was the image of some other she pursued in her responses, he could tell. He felt usurped, blasphemed, and grew morose when she accused him of possessiveness. There might have been violent scenes except that he was always slow to anger, afraid of what it might do, things said that could never be unsaid. He wanted to believe in the past, that there was a time, a place, when the miracle broke over them which now hung suspended, out of reach. She had shut him out. And fate, as if to balance the equation, in time evicted her from her niche.

For many years his mother had been a victim of multiple sclerosis and when she became confined to a wheelchair and unable to look after herself, he took her in. He could not find it in his heart to put her into care. Doors had to be widened, the brick path pointed up, a bedroom made downstairs, taps adjusted. Beth viewed the upheaval with horror and depression, appalled at the evidence of disability.

"Why do you have to be a martyr?" she attacked Adam.

"She *is* my mother."

"I *am* your wife."

He glanced at her with penetrating reproach. She had been unfaithful to him many times. "Yes," he said, "you are."

"She ought to be in a home, a place where she can have proper care."

"We can't afford it."

"It's too much for me to take on. There's Andrew to see to. He's very demanding these days. What sort of effect is it going to have on him, having an invalid around the house?"

Adam stared into the reddened coals. "I don't know. It's life, isn't it?"

There were moments when she wished she could crack his everlasting patience. She wouldn't need to feel so accused then. "Don't imagine that I can't see that you're doing this to punish me! She's all you have left. It's safer to spend your devotion on an invalid who's got no choice but to accept it. You won't be let down."

Silence filled the room. Then he said: "That may be true. She needs me nonetheless."

He sprang quietly from his chair and went out. She envied him his unwavering resolution. She felt cut in two when she saw how well he cared for his mother, gladly taking pains to ease her suffering, never faltering. She herself could only muster a spirit of grudging tolerance and let fly when the old lady knocked over a bowl of soup. Perhaps she had never loved Adam so honestly as the day she went off with Andrew to the swings and bought him Jelly Tots and a 60p aeroplane and didn't come back. Adam found the note propped up on his typewriter, crumpled it slowly and opened it again, searching the sky for an answer to his need to have and to hold. His mother called from the other room.

The following Friday, as she had promised, Elizabeth came back for her belongings. She drove up to the door in a silver saloon, slim as a bullet. She wore a red-spotted scarf tied peasant-fashion under her dark hair. She told him she was staying with her cousin in St. John's Wood. They'd always got on well. It was ideal really, Karen was an air stewardess and the flat stood unoccupied half the time. He wondered at this dubious facility for fitting into other people's lives. "You can't leave," he said impotently. "You can't just walk out. Look, why don't we sit down and discuss this like grown-ups?"

"And I'll be able to take up my painting again. It's a ground floor flat and there's a conservatory for my studio. It's so cramped here."

His tongue clove to the roof of his mouth. He did not know how to reach her. He ran distraught fingers through his well-groomed hair so that it flashed across her mind in an off-guard moment that he looked as appealingly unkempt as when he made love. "What about the boy?" he protested. "He is my son too."

"You can't have it both ways, Adam," she rejoined in a trenchant voice. She was  staring at the floor, her teeth gritted. There was a 1/2p piece on the carpet, half-camouflaged by the pattern. After several seconds she trusted herself to meet his gaze. "You've no time for him, that's certain. He needs *me*."

It was incredible how, in the space of twenty-five minutes she had removed all trace of herself and the child from the house. There were only the Ribena stains on the wall and the abandoned cot. "I shan't bother to send for that," Elizabeth said. "He's old enough to do without it." At the flat, she surrounded his bed with pillows in case he fell out in the night. It was not so much that he might do himself harm, bodies were supple at that age, but that he made such an awful din, the floorboards shook like an earthquake. Adam looked around the room denuded of infant paraphernalia. Even the poster with the bear in sou'wester and red wellingtons disappeared. It had the name of a station on it.

"Perhaps if you'd been able to share him... " Adam went on bitterly. He was watching her in panic, alert to further disaster. It was true that babies bewildered him. He felt clumsy handling the child and had been glad to let Elizabeth get on with it. She knew by instinct what to do. But deep within him was a well of indescribable tenderness and a need to impress his own destiny on the next generation. Elizabeth did not appreciate that. "He'll forget me, won't he? It will be as though I never existed."

Adam's eyes were brilliant as though from some implosion of torment. He had never been able to offload his anger, let others bear burdens for him. Long ago his mother had advised him to prune the pear tree against the side wall, but Elizabeth had objected. It was an unnatural thing to do, she said. In any case it bore little fruit, facing due north as it did, only eroded the pointing as neglect took hold and choked from memory its true function. *He'll forget me.*

Beth said: "You can come on Sundays if you like."

He was within touching distance of an answer. He could see bits of green, the bare contours of the golf course rising behind the houses on the other side of the road. Then his gaze settled upon her, hooded with despair. She was cramming toys into the boot of the car. "You know I can't. Who'll look after mother?"

The boot lid went down with a muffled slam. "You'll work something out," she said confidently. "I'll be off, then." She went round to the driver's door, mules slapping against her heels. The car took off and turned left at the end of the road; sun glanced off the rear window and sent a blinding ache across his vision. He had grown too used to the dim light of winter.

How long he stood there, immobile, torn between the claims of the future and the claims of the past, he did not know, but a sharp blast from a motorist's horn brought him to himself and he realised he was standing in the middle of the road. He made for the house, half-staggering, all feeling gone from his limbs. He was in possession of nothing but a resonant emptiness. It was as if flesh and bone were dissolving in some undilute emotion stronger than death from which there was no hope of deliverance. But a bright article caught his eye, for lying there on the tarmac was Andrew's golly. He picked it up and stared into its black, zany face with the permanent smile. For days it sat propped up on the kitchen windowsill, but one night Adam woke and thought of the child crying for what he had lost and next morning packed it up and sent it off in the post.

That summer most of the garden disappeared under concrete. Adam found it as hard to contend with the flowers as the weeds. The grass grew tall and the neighbourhood cats stalked one another like tigers in tropical undergrowth. Spaces were left here and there, just enough for a few hardy roses and shrubs.

Two years elapsed and then, just before Christmas, on the darkest day of the year, old Mrs Goodfellow passed away and with her his reason for living. He did not touch her room for weeks, but left it to gather dust, an odour of rotting flowers about the altar of her bed.

Adam slept badly during the weeks that followed and woke around four in the morning, dismayed that another day had dawned, afraid of its empty wastes. His body was charged with a feverish apprehension and broke into mechanical activity of its own accord. He could not remember having done anything or where he was when rinsed milk bottles were returned to the porch. He worried constantly about the price of bread and butter and soap, whether he ought to be investing in some cholesterol-lowering alternative and how he would stretch his income to cover the basic necessities of life. The insurance money would not go far – it had been taken out in an era of simple faith, when prices were modest and values were high – and he had worked only fitfully in recent months.

He was anxious about Andrew too. On occasion he had gone to St. John's Wood, calling in an agency nurse to sit with his mother. He did not enjoy going. The flat had an air of subterfuge and gilded lies. It had white-louvred fittings and Hockney and Warhol prints on the walls. The soft furnishings reeked of decaying perfume and a particularly acrid foreign tobacco. The place was so airless always. He loosened his black cravat until Elizabeth, seeing his panic, offered to open a window and gave him a drink. She herself was so sensitive to draughts.

Andrew was overjoyed by these visits. He was a delightful child with zircon-blue eyes and thick fronds of toffee-blond hair. He brought toys and laid them at Adam's feet, climbed on to his knee and burrowed in his pockets for the chocolate buttons which were sure to be there, feeding Adam as many as he ate himself. It was not without a prick of envy that Elizabeth observed a certain magic between father and son, but, emulating her, the boy called him Adam, a habit she made no attempt to correct. If Adam was hurt, at least it satisfied his artistic ear and seemed to confirm his role of being at a remove from the action. Once Elizabeth spoke of divorce, but there was no tact or premeditation in her manner. It was as though she acted on demon impulse and was trying to goad him into some affronted response. He did not take her up, although, afterwards, he debated whether access to the child might not be made more natural were the situation put on a legal footing. He even wondered whether it would be possible to gain custody and how much that would affect Andrew. But he could not face the endless wranglings of the court. It was an admission of what he preferred not to admit. No more was said, however.

Well, that time was over and gone. He had made a clean break with the past and come north of the Border to the open country he loved where a man might still fancy himself a pioneer. Here he realised his long-cherished dream of running a bookshop. The business flourished. Andrew was at prep school midway between London and Perth and came to stay in the holidays. These were intensely happy weeks for both of them. He called Adam 'Dad' and they went fishing together for rock salmon and cooked sausages over a fire, and Adam, bending over the boy's shoulder, guiding his hand as he reeled in the line, thought he would never again be as close to another human being as this.

Mrs Craig, she who 'did' for Mr Oliphant at the manse, never far from a motherless bairn, brought round homemade shortbread and cheese scones for these expeditions. She clasped the boy to her bosom, cried: *Och! How he's grown! Andrew, 'tis a fine Scots name, that, a name to be proud of. Twas Craig's middle name and he was the best!* It was always the same, the words were proclaimed in the same spirit of lyric discovery. If Andrew shuffled a bit with embarrassment, he devoured the scones with great relish and thought her a pretty good sort. Adam smiled his smile of genuine pleasure, a watery film lit his slanting eyes so that you did not know whether it was a trick of the light or if he had just come in from the cold. He understood so many things now, above all other people's suffering. He had an affinity with those who had taken sorrow into their stride. He was profoundly thankful to have pursued his lifeline. *Well, Andrew with the fine Scots name, won't you ask Mrs Craig to stay to tea?*

Aye, I'll bide a wee while, little mannie, for when God made time, He made plenty of it!

Looking back, Adam did not know how circumstances could have been different. He simply wished they had been.

He wished he had been wiser and hadn't taken it for granted that Elizabeth loved him as much as he loved her. Such fantastic economies were not of this world. People changed, showed other facets, were elusive. He would have gone to the ends of the earth for her while she sought him in the avenue off the North Circular Road. Remembering those times, especially the early days, he seemed to be watching a former self. How alien the habits of intimacy were to him now, how dried out and set in his ways he had become. He had no desire to relive what was gone, but he knew that something precious was lost to him for ever.

Adam could not settle with his pipe and his books on the evening of the trip to Kintully Castle. He enjoyed sitting by the fire with the wind moaning over the moors while he allowed himself excursions in prose. To and fro he went in the house, putting things away in drawers, shifting piles of books that got under his feet. He didn't know why they hadn't bothered him before. Yesterday's article was tossed into the wastebasket. His approach was too stale, it lacked verve. He made tea and forgot to drink it. In the shop, by the last light, he read Esther's note about that afternoon's trade, unusually brisk it had been, but the news failed to gladden him. It all seemed so distant, so *unnecessary*.

And then it took hold of him, *accidie* black as pitch. His life was a millwheel plunging endlessly through the same tracts of waste water. Its safe tenor had mesmerised him. Maybe what he needed was adventure, a challenge. He'd go and see Logan at the travel agent's first thing in the morning. Maybe they could offer a cruise around the Greek Islands, or he might join a 'dig' in some desert place and rediscover the joys of probing an earlier civilisation. But he couldn't project himself into that frame of mind. He did not want to go back *there*. He hadn't been away for a holiday since he'd lived in Glenfinnie, hadn't felt the need of one, wedded to his work and this land as he was.

The minutes ticked by and the feeling loosened its hold. In its wake a wave of inspiration came rinsing through him. His thoughts flew to his writing and the latest piece on Gaelic lore. Lucid phrases began to spill through his mind, his ears rang with their cadences, familiar and true, and he made for his desk, fumbling in the dark for the light switch. The bulb pinged and went out in a flash. But he sat down and wrote, line upon line in the dark, watched the quaver and lilt of the larch tree outside, dense black against the paler dark of the sky. It stirred now and then and lapsed into motionless ease. And a presence stole over him, filling the room, for a brief moment exposing him to an eternity of sadness and exquisite pain, and he turned round fully thinking to see her there. "Angel?" There was nothing but charged space. She was gone from him and had come back in some strange immaterial way, stronger yet that her physical self, as loved ones returned to the bereaved. And when those moments had also passed he felt comforted to have her there, resting in the quiet of himself while the timbre of her voice became linked with the whispering night.

He went to bed content and slept soundly for three or four hours.

He awoke, shivering, to find the quilt heaped on the floor and a vigorous draught slicing through the room. The wind was in an odd direction, coming full tilt through the open transom. He swung out of bed and pulled the window to. It was stiff. He seldom closed it summer or winter, disliking the atmosphere to grow torpid and stale. He pulled the quilt back on to the bed, drew it up and tried to shut out life and its claims. A warm glow surrounded him, but each time he began to drift into sleep, he kept jolting awake. The draught had grown high-pitched and imperative since its exclusion. It whined around the windowframe like a dog pleading for admission.

At length, he heaved himself on to his back and stared up at the ceiling. His thoughts reverted to yesterday and the tea-shop, smelling of applewood and toast, where a fire shone in copper kettles and pans. Angel had admired the spinning-wheel in the corner. Did he know that beautiful spinning-wheel song, Irish she believed it to be? Yes, he said, he knew it, had even endeavoured to play it on the harp, woman's instrument though it was. An Italian Contessa had bequeathed it to his mother and he couldn't bring himself to part with it.

Angel had been a little amused by that. "So you are musical," she had said and had *blushed*.

"I'll show you next time you come," he had promised.

"Would you?"

"It's a bit out of tune..."

"Don't your fingers get calloused?"

"They do if you practise long hours, which I don't. I've a Steinway, you see. I play that a touch better. It's in an upper room, along with the harp, and getting it there was no mean feat, I can tell you."

"May I come and listen to you play?"

"Yes, I should like that. I should like to play something especially for you. What shall it be? A Mozart sonata?"

She had smiled and nodded slowly, as though conceding a point. It was rare to feel so in tune with herself. "As long as there's Mozart, I can bear anything."

Perhaps it was then that the note of discord had been struck, so natural and in place at the time, in retrospect so disquieting. Angel's eyes were fixed on a point beyond the room, though there was no view to speak of, not from where they were. *What was it about her?*

Outside, the lone wheep of a lapwing; the fair light of dawn breaking faith with the night. Day was coming. There was no going back to the dark.

Though he chose still to resist, Adam *knew*.


"I wish you hadn't to go back to an empty house," I'd said

to Adam before we parted. "I wish there was someone to care for you."

He had watched me vanish between the vapour-hung firs. Most of the house was hidden from view. It looked eerie. One might have imagined a dark spirit lurking there, chafing against captivity. I heard him restart the engine and drive off as I rounded the curve at the top of the drive and came upon the vermilion streak that was Jude's new car. Not built for the roads of Britain, he'd said, but an asset, nevertheless. A lamp was on low in the drawing-room and the curtains undrawn. He moved away from the window at my approach, his shadow flying, distorted, across the wall.

And so it was I who came in fresh from the world, its emanations aglow in my countenance. "Jude?" I unfastened my coat. The atmosphere in the room rejected me. An empty Glenlivet bottle stood on the coffee table.

"Where have you been?"

"I left a message. On the dresser. Didn't you see it?" I said lightly.

"Yes, I read it."

"Well, then…"

"I came home early. Something vital's come up. I came home to tell you but you weren't here. You're never *there* when I want you."

"I'm sorry I'm not where you want me to be."

"Out with a stranger!"

I took a deep breath and closed my eyes for a second. The day had evaporated. The dark firs linked arms against the sky and I longed for the larch at the heart of the town. I wanted to be there instead of here on this lonely hill where no one came except to lay flowers on the graves of those who were gone and maybe to the service every other Sunday. "Jude, I have to talk to you. We must talk."

"How long have you known him?" Jude demanded. He took another bottle from the cabinet, breaking the seal with a flick of his wrist.

"Do you have to keep drinking that stuff," I protested. "Don't you think you've had enough?"

"It makes the world a more convivial place, gives the illusion of company."

"You encouraged me to go out and meet people."

"You haven't even mentioned him."

What was it he feared from the stranger, I wondered, as he stood apart from me so that I could see his shadow and his reflection at once? I couldn't help thinking of Marilyn. The note was screwed up in the hearth, having missed the grate by a couple of inches. How wearisome that the accent should fall in the wrong place, that scraps of paper should become so invested with meaning.

"I didn't think you could have any objection."

"Well, I have," Jude snapped. "You might have introduced me."

"Yes," I said. For so I might. "It didn't occur to me that you'd be interested."

For it was inconceivable that I could have covered the same ground with Jude I had covered with Adam. That we should have climbed the ascent in order to gaze not at the view, but a piece of the mountain itself.

Jude was sitting, bent over, his arms resting loosely across his knees, staring at the carpet. When he spoke it was with a mere sideways cast of the head, almost as if he were addressing my feet. "It was nothing...with Marilyn," he said in a deflated tone. "An aberration. I kept thinking of you."

"Why did you come home early?"

Jude huffed. "Kaufmann, the German chemical firm, have made an offer for us. A very attractive one. It's been on the cards for some weeks. Apparently, they're looking to broaden their interests in Britain."

I was startled. "What will it mean?"

"That's what I intend to find out. I'm flying to Munich in the morning. Tomorrow, who knows, we may be as good as part of the great Kaufmann empire." He tossed off his drink.

"Meredith's threat of resigning was certainly timely. He'd been got at, I see that now."

"I don't understand."

"It turns out that Raven's family have an interest in Kaufmann. I knew that Judas wasn't to be trusted."

I made an effort to organise my thoughts. Even now circumstances seemed to be militating against me. "Will Meredith stay if you go ahead?"

"If the terms are right. It's exactly what he was gunning for, an opening with dazzling prospects. If not, the compensation will probably be generous."

"When will you be back?"

"The following day. Thursday, if all goes according to plan. They're only prelim talks."

"By then you'll know which direction to take."

Jude gave a tense, defeated sigh. "I'm in a cleft stick. I can't deny that at present to accept would solve some of our problems." He got up and moved to the sceneless window. "When I think of all the talent and energy that's been poured into the business, my father, his father before him…"

"Yes."

"It was my lifeline. Today, I suddenly saw how it had been for you all these months. Losing the baby. Giving up your job. The future swept away. Then you were thrust into life up here, away from friends and all that was familiar. Not just the bitter disappointment, but the fact that a process had started and not…finished. You just had to bear it."

"I'm glad… I'm glad you saw that."

"You must have felt bereft."

"He was almost old enough to have lived, our baby. If it had happened a week or two later…"

I think Jude knew what I meant, that by a hair's breadth one could fail to reach Canaan. He had dreamed of an heir in the days when he saw a brilliant future unfurling over the horizon and himself the strongest link in the chain.

"Don't. Don't torment yourself thinking about it."

"I should like you to have had a son. Someone. It wouldn't be so bad, then."

"There'll be others," he said flatly.

And, of course, for him it could well be true. He would marry again, the years would pass. My life with him would be no more than an interlude.

"I can't... I'm never going to have children..." I faltered. "They told me some while ago. I'm not well, you see... *It's never going to get better.*"

Jude came towards me. He put his arms around me but he might have been consoling a stranger. I felt him braced against some force he would not admit. "They told you? They didn't tell me. They would have done surely."

"I didn't want them to. I wanted to tell you myself when the time was right."

"But why...?" he persisted in a stricken voice. "Have I been so far away from you?"

Relief swept over me. The raging moment of impact I had dreaded didn't occur. It had paid off after all to allow the situation to take its course. Now I'd be able to help him cope with any manifestation of delayed shock.

"You've been so taken up since we came to this place."

"Nothing's gone right. I was thinking before you came in that I'd like to strip off all the wallpaper and start again. I'll bring you some sample books, you could choose new designs. We could refurbish the whole house...!"

Momentarily, I was carried along with him as I had been in the old days, glad and sad both, my hopes rising on a wave of euphoria. "You could tackle the garden first."

He took both my hands and looked into my face, yet not searching there, for his head was promptly filled with visions of its own and the whisky fumes were strong upon his breath. "Can't you see?" he cried. "It won't any of it matter twelve months from now!"

The power ebbed for a split second. The lamp flickered. I realised that he hadn't understood. I thought I had overstated the case, that the truth must be transparent, but he hadn't understood! He had merely wished to allay my fears on his behalf that he couldn't have sons.

"It's getting late," he said. "I must go and pack. I'm leaving before dawn." Stupefied, I watched him disappear through the door I'd left open on the way in. "I'll have the spare room tonight," he called down the stairs, "then I shan't disturb you first thing."


That night I dreamt of a great forest, firs and larches together, under a glistening weight of snow. You couldn't tell which was which unless the white burden slithered away and a bough sprang up light and free. I was drifting above it. The air was thin with the scent of resin and keen as a weapon. This untrodden wilderness was boundless, pricked with spectral tones. The eye sought in vain for relief. Far off, plumes of smoke issued into the sky, perhaps from a woodsman's fire. It was pleasant to the senses, smelling of refuge and the revived complicity of the afternoon. But as I drew closer, its character changed. I became aware of its acrid taint, increasing in volume until the full force of its billowing heat spent itself upon me. I came upon a tortured wreckage of metal, trees felled like blades of grass, limbs, shoes and tomorrow's newspapers fetched up in branches a mile or more away; numbers prophesied in the gaping mouths of passports. The sight of that dislocated data brought a prickle to my flesh. Long ago I had divined in the sinister shape of aircraft a means of coming to grief. Down it had come, a grotesque silver bird, wings shattered, the warm throb of life severed for good. Since the age of seven, I'd been acquainted with all the hope and joy that preceded calamity. I wanted to turn back, shed my eyes, do anything in expiation of such an offence. Better to drift above an earth hidebound by its snowlit vision than this. But there was no regaining the innocent perception of children secure in a garden as wide as the sky. This was the obscene truth and my entire being recoiled in terror and gathered itself into a scream I could not deliver.

I woke. The room was bathed in light. For a while I lay unconscious of my surroundings while the horror of dreaming prevailed. All was quiet. Offbeam shadows trembled on the ceiling. Something wasn't right. The door was closed. Last night the door had been open. I peered at my watch. Five minutes to ten! I sprang out of bed, and making a grab for the door, rushed across the landing "Jude!"

There was no answer. Nothing stirred in the room. Panting wildly, I leaned against the wall, its coldness striking through my thin nightwear. The chaos of the unmade bed strewn with discarded items of clothing echoed the dream. The scene of that clearing created by disaster swam up before me and I knew that this was a silence I would never learn to endure, not in this world or the next. It was too late!

The telephone startled me. I had to think where it was. I made my way towards it and groped for the receiver. "Adam?"

"Angel? Are you all right?"

"What? Yes, yes, I'm all right."

"You sound distant, strained."

"I… I overslept."

"Oh dear, did I wake you?"

"No."

"I'm coming round," he said. There was a moment's pause. "May I come round?"

"Yes, please. Give me a few moments to shower and dress."

I had left the door ajar and was halfway down the stairs when he came in and held out his arms as if tacitly pledged to take me up where I most wanted to be. I was soothed. All is well, I thought, as Mother Julian of Norwich had averred all those centuries ago. Everything that was good and right-minded had been held in abeyance. The rest I shrugged off like the bad dream it was.

"What is it?"

"A piece of nonsense," I said, forcing a brightness I did not feel. "Will you join me for breakfast?"

"Why not?" he said amiably. "It's five hours since I had mine." And catching my quizzical glance: "I didn't sleep well."

I set down a bowl of fruit on the table, laid a place for him there, and one for myself. I made coffee and brought honey and marmalade and toast. Wholewheat, I told him. I made it myself!

"Adam, are you superstitious?"

He frowned. He was watching the blade of the breadknife poised on the loaf's crust. "It depends what you mean. Not about Friday the thirteenth and walking under ladders."

"The power of telepathy, for instance. Auguries. The principle Jung called 'synchronicity'. Don't you sometimes feel that all our actions of part of a gigantic equation that has to be satisfied?"

He cut a corner of butter. "As a matter of fact, yes I do. But you'd be treading on thin ice to try and construe every suggestion of the paranormal."

"It's the dream I had... I can't get it out of my head."

"About what?"

"An air crash in a *Bavarian* forest. Could it be guilt, do you think?"

Our eyes met. He said nothing, but bent his head to drink coffee so that I would have given much to retract my misgivings. "You don't talk about your husband."

"We seem to be pursuing separate lives. All his energies are geared to expansion, the building of empires. I like to take life at a more leisurely pace. I'm scared I'll miss something important if I don't."

"I see," Adam responded thoughtfully, with that peculiar absence which brought his presence closer. "Yes, I do see that." He said he had noticed the Harmony Colophon of stylised treble and bass clef.

"You shouldn't have done it," I accused him from under my lashes.

"What shouldn't I have done?"

"Hidden that book under the counter the way you did."

"Would it have made any difference?"

"I don't know. If I hadn't come back…"

"I didn't hide it in any case, not in the first instance. It was an accident. They do happen, you know."

"That's what I mean." I caught a faint wail of foreboding in the words.

"Look, don't stay here all by yourself today. Come back with me."

I glanced at the draining board with its empty dish from an earlier breakfast. "I don't know."

"I could do with a hand if you wouldn't mind helping. It's Esther's afternoon off and I've to mind the shop and prepare next month's catalogue. We've a mailing list all over the world."

Adam's mood was one of muted rapture at having me upon his own turf as he went soft-footing about. I'd look up from describing the condition of volumes for sale from a list of abbreviations he had given me, and he would be watching, that minute gleam in his eye.

We worked for the rest of the morning and well into the afternoon when we went into the garden for lunch, or maybe it was tea. It was such a contrast to ours at Linden Hill, a retreat brought to perfection in sequences of flush growth. "Who'd dream this was here behind these stone walls?" I said. "Even from the windows you can't tell it's like this." There were areas of half-tamed wilderness starred with wood-sorrel and rhododendrons the soft hue of heather, birch saplings rippling against evergreens. Soon there'd be azaleas, wisteria, and dahlias, later, when the seedlings were hardened off and transplanted. "Ah dahlias," Adam reflected. "I look forward to September for them. When summer is fading, the garden's blazing with colour."

He led me to a bower where we could sit and brought out smoked salmon sandwiches and a bottle of champagne he'd had in for ages for a special occasion. We were in frolicsome spirits as the cork winced out of the neck and exploded. I held up my glass to the smouldering orifice, let the liquid light rise close to the brim. The sun poured down a golden heat, filtering into the crevices of the stonework. No one rang the shop bell.

After closing time, he took me up to the attic room where his Steinway was and the old harp handed on by his mother's friend, the Contessa. It was thick with dust standing naked in a corner with one of its strings broken. But he played a few chords and made the dust fly. The old magic came. I knew I was honoured to have been brought to this sanctuary where very few trod. I began to sing as I'd sung on the shores of the loch on the first visit to Scotland. *Plaisir d'Amour*. My voice had lost its clear tone from lack of use and imperfect health. But he continued to play, the song and the melody blending together, flawed but harmonious.

"It must be the champagne," I said, abashed, when we came to the end. "People don't do such things."

"As Hedda Gabler observed."

Adam forsook the harp and went over to the piano, sinking down on the velvet stool with a dejected air. His fingers wandered at random over the keys until some semblance of a tune emerged. It happened to be *Für Elise*.

"She shot herself, didn't she?"

"Who? Hedda? It was the only way…"

On top of the piano were two silver-framed photographs, one of a small boy of seven or eight in school uniform, an expression of bashful chagrin on his impish face, the other of a stunning, sable-haired beauty, self-willed and temperamental, with huge olive-dark eyes. There was a look of eldritch humour in them.

"My wife," Adam explained, "and my son."

"I knew there must be someone...someone like this," I said, daring to lift the portrait gently.

"Why did you feel that, I wonder?"

"Because...it informs all that you do."

"We've been separated for nine years or so. I haven't seen her for two. We talk on the phone occasionally."

"Separated?"

"We're not divorced. Elizabeth no longer holds with marriage so the question of divorce doesn't arise."

"But surely..."

"She's living in Hampstead. In an artists' commune or something of the sort. I don't like Andrew going there, but they have a right to see each other. Fortunately, he's away at school a lot of the time. Or here with me."

"Elizabeth. Haven't I heard of Elizabeth Goodfellow? Isn't she a famous artist?"

"Yes, you'll have heard of her. She exhibits all over Europe and in New York. More style than substance. She's become popular since she went her own way."

"But it is your name by which she is known."

At this gentle irony, his solemn face melted into a smile, the humour creases extending across his temples. The trace of defensiveness died in his voice. "I have two of her pictures," he mused, "the only mementoes she left behind. I don't think she thought it worth coming back. Now they would fetch a great deal of money. It would run into four or five figures any day of the week."

He was restored, though not by any invention of mine.

"Adam, I must go. Thank you for today. Thank you for *rescuing* me."

He sprang off the stool, his gaze working rapidly. "You mustn't leave now. You can't go back to that house and be alone."

"It's my home. It's where I belong."

"So today was just a Fool's Paradise?"

"Presently I shall be tired and very poor company."

"If you want to rest, you can rest here. I won't disturb you. I'll creep around as quietly as I can."

"Adam... don't," I pleaded. "It's difficult enough as it is." My left hand was caught between both of his as I turned to go.

"Please... I feel *responsible*."

Instinct rebelled against reducing him to a beggary his stance was so ill-fitted to bear. "If you like, I'll cook supper for you later. Come round about eight."

"Very well, I'll do that," he agreed with an air of great courtesy. "Thank you."

I made my way home across the tangled heather, a short cut I'd discovered not long go. The air was tense and magnetic.

At five past eight, Adam arrived on the doorstep. The first lightning streaked the gloom. Spots of rain rebounded off the bushes by the door, followed by a distant pang of thunder.

"Looks as though we're in for a pretty grim night," he forecast.

I led him into the drawing-room where the fire had settled down to a steady flicker. He said what a welcome sight it was, much pleasanter than the three kilowatt he generally resorted to these days. I switched on the lamps and tugged at the curtain cords to shut out the weather. I wanted to forget that backcloth of thorns and thistles where the lawns should have been. Having seen Adam's garden, I was freshly appalled at the state of our own. Only last week, Jude had remarked how pretty some of the gardens were in Glenfinnie. *"They've a good tilth of soil down there in the town. Up here you're contending with solid rock."*

During supper, rain slithered in torrents over the panes. We could hear a gale getting up. It shook the windows and drew the candle flames into the slipstream of the draught so that the house seemed a frail defence against the storm.

We spoke as acquaintances rather than friends, warily edging our way anew, with an almost exaggerated politeness, into knowledge of one another. Afterwards, while I was making coffee in the kitchen, Adam flicked through some discs and withdrew Mozart's *Flute and Harp Concerto* because he felt sufficiently armed to exorcise old ghosts. The work had been his passion at the time Elizabeth had attended his Byzantine lectures and he first got to know her. Since then he'd discovered Wagner, Mahler and Stravinsky as forces giving expression to his frame of mind and had shunned the poignant strains of Mozart whose recurring themes had so betrayed him. So it was in a spirit of forgiveness and a readiness to admit that the *ancien régime* had played a natural part in his development that he turned to the work again.

"I'm afraid this one is the worse for wear," I said.

"The storm isn't helping."

We lapsed into a reticent ease, listening, unwilling to disturb the frequency. The music moved effortlessly along, imposing its regular metre on the disorder outside, overriding the rumble of thunder which caused the joists to vibrate. The plaintive vigour of the flute flirted, danced, interleaved with the mellow ripple of the harp playing like light in a depth of sunlit water.

"I suppose," I said, somewhat languidly, when it came to an end and my coffee stood cold, "we ought to switch off the power. We're vulnerable as high as this."

"I can't leave you," he said. "It's so isolated here. The house could be plunged into darkness at any minute."

The rain beat down relentlessly on to the patio. It gushed from clogged gutterspouts and cut a way into the drain with a sound as clear and sonorous as the bubbling burn. "I couldn't send you out into the weather, not since you're here," I said. "Why did you come? You shouldn't have come. You should have done the honourable thing and refused."

"I came because you needed me...and I you."

Put like that it sounded so right, for what government, what ministry, could have contrived so fine an economy?

What exchequer with an eye on the bottom line could make ends meet to such advantage? How could it be wrong to deploy resources where they were most needed? It had nothing to do with what was 'rotten in the state', the bankruptcy of Britain, the world, the rise and descent of Indices, values fluctuating day by day so that all sense of priority went to the wall, did it? In any case, one would require greater vanity than Canute to hope to stem the tide single-handed.

Our hands touched, linked, and I last I succumbed to the unbearable tension of longing to be embraced and to meet him where he was most vulnerable, wherever that be. "Come to bed," I whispered. The pins slid from my topknot and my hair slowly uncoiled and slithered down to become entangled with kisses. I melted into the sweet sadness him, taking on, as it were, his yoke of bitterness. Oh, the slaking it was for us both to find one another, isolated, parched as we had been on our mental plane for so long.

Yet... yet... I heard the echo of unplumbed depths, scented the power of welded destinies. Unbidden, the lost aura of the nightmare superimposed itself and I fancied, was it real or imagined, that I could smell burning? The fire had been left unguarded downstairs. The whole house might set alight while I took flight in dalliance! My flesh tensed and contracted. I was suddenly fearful of the point we had reached, our needs inextricably bound up together. The day I perceived him in the doorway quicksands shifted under my feet. I knew him, every predestined line of him, the unique assemblage of his limbs. Adam who was the sky and the earth and the wind sighing through the glen. Who would have guessed that it was for him I would die?

For if lovemaking meant anything, it had to mean everything, and how could I give what was already contracted out? I was looking to him to underwrite a double deficit, his own and mine, and mine encumbered with death. "Oh Adam! Oh Christ! I don't want to die!"

And that was the truth so long in coming. For months I had slammed the door in its face. At last it broke through and stormed the house.

The light went out. The power had gone. The lines must have come down as he'd predicted. This uncivilised place! This savage, beautiful terrain north of the Border!

"What do you mean?" he asked in a strange, searching voice, half-shielding himself from a reply. Slowly, he relaxed his grip.

"I... They tell me I haven't long left. Heart problems. I won't make it through the next bout of 'flu."

Silence. "Is there no hope at all?" he said.

"Save some sort of miracle. Lourdes is a long way. If I went, Jude would have to know."

"He doesn't know?"

"If he did, I'd have no life left."

"But he deserves the truth, doesn't he? "

"I don't know how to tell him," I sobbed. "He won't *understand*."


The thunder had rolled away. Clouds scudded across the sky on some reckless errand of their own. Rain dripped from the trees sifting down through the leaves with the sound of a bird taking flight.

At a quarter to five the power was restored and the light came on. Angel did not stir. It was daybreak. Adam felt a strong urge to be by himself, to walk on the howe in the dying storm with the wind in his face and the feel of things that went on for ever. For though she nestled so trustingly against his breast, he knew that he must let her go. He might pour out his soul to comfort her, but he was powerless to bear her fate. Gently disentwining himself, he drew up the covers around her. Then, after scribbling a brief note, he went from the house as noiselessly as he'd entered the shop to find her his next customer, a lifetime ago.

I awoke uneasily to the faraway sound of knocking, as if someone outside besought me to open the door. A maple branch was tapping in a fine staccato against the eaves. The wind must have changed course.

Gulls circled above in fathomless blue, drifting on thermals. After the watershed of last night, there was a sense of restoration, of things acknowledged and in their right place. It had been part of the not-telling, my dismissal of the body, every bit, in its way, as treacherous as Jude's neglect of the spirit.

Then I remembered. The *whole* situation. The pieces fell into place with a kind of lucid integrity. Adam and Jude, Marilyn, myself. Elizabeth...

I rolled over and my eye aligned to the note Adam had left on the pillow. The sheer inadequacy of human nature, adding caustic to wounds it set out to heal!

*I'll be back,* it read.

Suddenly, a heartbroken sob shook me. My hands flew to cover my face. Long tears trickled down between my fingers. I would never know the precious experience of surfacing from sleep, through broken sighs, to the profound security of Adam's arms.

The tapping continued unendurably.


At eleven-o-clock I heard footsteps approaching. He appeared at the door, haggard, drawn, distracted, his hair clawed by the wind. He had on no overcoat, just his jacket with the collar turned up. He looked lost and bewildered, a man who has roamed round in circles and stumbled by accident on the starting point.

"Come on in and get warm. You look perished," I said.

"I decided... if I could get away it would be all right. But there's nowhere to go."

"I'll make you some coffee." I made him toast and scrambled eggs too, which seemed to give nourishment without his knowledge.

At last, I mustered some resolution. "Listen, Adam, you must go home and try to pick up the threads. Compel yourself to go through your daily routine until it has meaning again."

"How can there be any meaning? How can it matter?"

"Anodyne toil, remember?"

"Stones made bread?"

"Oh, if only there were someone back home to take care of you and give point to your life! I shall pray to Our Lady for that. A man like you should not be alone." I opened his palm to plant a kiss there. "These hands need someone to work for, to cherish." I turned from him. "Please go now. I'll come and see you sometimes."

"Will you? Will you do that? It isn't goodbye, then?"

"It will never be that. What we have is for keeps. Life has to go on. Only we sometimes mistake what it is."


But if he had lost the whole world, Adam hardly knew whether he had gained his own soul.

The accounts were piling up on his desk. Esther had left them for him to deal with, as was their procedure. Fuel bills, rates, publishers' invoices. The rent too had gone up. In a frenzy of pure frustration, he determined to seek other premises. It was out of the question to subsist in cramped quarters with such exorbitant overheads, albeit at the centre of town.

He strove to apply himself to work, to simulate the conditions of yesterday, but it wasn't yesterday. Yesterday, Angel was with him. The garden was blooming and had leapt out at his famished gaze with vibrant clarity. They had laughed together in the sun. How could she laugh, knowing that we die? Now, when he ventured out there, questing after what he had lost, it was a place of dry bones and dereliction. If it went on for ever, it went on with a will of its own. He knew of old the infidelity of spring. He followed the stone insets going past the arbour and down to the incinerator where he burnt brash every winter. And he knew he would bear it. He would go on living here. This was his foothold in the land he loved. Having had his vision, he would settle for what he possessed.

The trouble was that even when his mind seemed steadfastly on the new catalogue, the pain would seep through. So it was, in a way, an answer to prayer when the turn of events that afternoon pitchforked him into action. He switched on the radio as a distraction, but it might have been off for all the heed he paid it.

It was during a newsflash, while he was sharpening a pencil, that he started and froze as though touched on the shoulder. "Reports are coming in of an air crash in Germany earlier today. The plane, a Jumbo Jet, flight No. BA 407, bound for Heathrow, came down only minutes after take-off in a forest area on the outskirts of Munich. It is not yet known how many survivors there are among the 291 passengers, but the pilot and crew are believed to have been killed. Over to our reporter, Felix Ryder, at Franz Joseph Strauss Airport..."

Adam seized the remote control and flicked on the television. There on the screen, in front of the newscaster, was a broad red band with information travelling across it. He found the cordless and punched out the number as he watched, anxious to confirm that it was someone else's disaster. A woman answered. Her voice was cool and efficient, not entirely dispassionate. It had none of the muted urgency of the newshound. He told her he had just learnt of the crash and was making enquiries on behalf of the family of Mr Jude Brightman who was believed to have been booked on the flight. She said, *Bear with me a moment.* There was some clicking at the other end and the hum of a commotion. *Thank you for holding.* Yes, Mr Brightman was booked on the flight but she was terribly sorry, there was no news of him as yet. He had not been accounted for. She took Adam's number and promised that next-of-kin would be informed as soon as there was news. *If I could make a note of your number,* she said.

He carefully replaced the receiver. It was eerie to be so intimately concerned about the fate of a person he didn't know, had never seen. He was trespassing on untrodden ground.

An hour and fifty-two minutes later, the telephone bleeped for the third time. He leapt to answer it on a surge of fresh hope and fear. There had been a further news bulletin calling the incident one of the worst in aviation history.

"Mr Goodfellow?" enquired the discarnate voice. Was it sanguine or grave? "We have news of Mr Brightman for you."

"Is he...?"

"It appears he has sustained a number of injuries and is being detained in the University of Munich Hospital."

"How bad is he? Do you know? What sort of injuries?"

"I'm afraid I can't help you there, though we'd have waited until Mrs Brightman was contacted had it been critical. I can give you the hospital number..."

Adam took it down, thanked her and rang off. He'd postponed telling Angel on the slim chance he'd be able to deliver good news along with the bad. If she'd already heard, she'd surely have been in touch. Clumsy German phrases bombarded his mind, a language he'd never used except as a tourist. He hoped he'd be able to make himself understood.

He poised the flat end of his pencil and pressed out the new number.

I went to the door fresh from sleep, surprised to see Adam for the second time that day and alerted by the look on his face. "Adam!"

"Perhaps you should sit down, Angel. I've some bad news, though heaven knows, it could be a lot worse."

"Bad news?" I repeated stupidly. "What's happened?"

"You were right. Your dream must have been an omen. There's been an aircrash."

It was all coming back to me, the horror of it. "Jude...!"

"He's in hospital, in Munich. I've been in touch with them. As far as they can say at the moment, he has concussion and a broken femur. He's as comfortable as can be expected. They spoke perfect English."

The walls began to tilt. I sank down on a stair. "I knew it," I cried, my head in my hands. "I knew he would come a cropper one day. I wanted to tell him. But it was too late."

"It wasn't your fault."

"He wouldn't have listened anyway."

"He's going to be all right. I'm sure he'll pull through."

"When did it happen?"

"Close on midday, they say."

"At midday? About the time you were leaving, then?"

In that instant, I felt myself emerge from a trance. Jude's sheepskin hung on the coat-rack, lifeless and yet so full of him. Strength was coming to me from somewhere.

"I'm going to him, Adam."

"Ought you to?"

"Yes, I must."

"Then I'm coming with you."


In next to no time my mother-in-law was on the line, pouring out a confused lament about her cavalier treatment of Jude. She hadn't meant to deny him, but he could be so obstructive, so stubborn.

I listened with impatience. My days of guilt and the championship of dubious causes were over and gone. The sound of Eudora's voice travelling over the miles between us seemed to emanate from regions I had long left behind.

"I'm flying out to him," I informed her.

""But, of course. I must come too. We must all go!"

"I don't suppose he'll be allowed many visitors."

"I *am* the poor boy's mother!"

"He is my husband."

"Well, perhaps it would be best. The young are so resilient."

"I'll be in touch with you as soon as I've news."

"Oh, my dear! Ring as often as you like while you're there. Feel free to reverse the charges!"


At the airport, awaiting the flight out, I observed the faces of those coming and going: genial, dour, expectant, disheartened, and thought that humanity was not as inimical as it had once appeared, but at the mercy of a tide more powerful than itself. It meant well.

"You're very composed," Adam said.

"I used to think," I said, "that it was better not to have what one couldn't keep, better never to know than to risk losing. Now I see how one can live on memories, the strength to be drawn from them. But one must be prepared to let go."


It was not as cheerless a place as I'd imagined, this city of cactus domes and attenuated gables, far away from the Scottish land and once the scene of doctrinaire persecutions. We came upon it by night in the plane, but next morning I woke to see how enchanting it was, a striking blend of ancient and modern influences set against the candescent spine of a mountain range.

The streets reverberated to the rise and fall of changed gears. The cosmopolitan scent of arabica coffee and *pumpernickel* wafted from bottle-glazed breakfast rooms and in the *Konditorei* displays of layered torte and Black Forest *kuchen* lavish with fresh fruit tempted the passer-by. The city was charged with anticipation, a foot in the old world and one in the new, and the hint of gold just around the corner.

Outdoors, the air was sharp as metal. Inside the hospital, the atmosphere struck a blow, taking the edge off our senses with its anaesthetic warmth. My heart beat thickly with renewed apprehension, cut off all at once from the flow of life as the heavy doors closed behind us. The language, too, was unnerving. Out there, its angular rhythms had been impersonal, all part of a pattern. Within, they fell hard on the ear, making demands I could not meet. I grappled with half-deciphered phrases but could not break into the flow, never having had more command than the average tourist. I stared around me mystified by the evidence of communication. Nor did it help that the doctor we spoke to, pale-eyed and imperturbable, had a heavy English accent.

Nevertheless, within a quarter of an hour a student nurse was leading us down a long corridor. "I'll wait for you here,"Adam said, touching my elbow. We went through more swing doors and into the ward where Jude was.

I could not tell whether he expected me or not. It was strange, seeing him there, a casualty among many. He was barely recognisable. His left leg was encased in plaster. His head was bound, his face pallid and bruised, the closed eyes receding into the skull.

"Jude…"

His lids parted narrowly. There was a glint of movement between the dark fringes of his lashes. Then he winced in an agony of remembrance. "You should not have come," he muttered.

The phrase had a certain resonance. "How do you feel?"

"My brain aches and aches. They can't make it stop. They can get to the moon, though."

I could not help smiling as he had meant me to do. For now he was a true giver of gifts. In weakness and indisposition he lent his support as he had not been able to do from the vantage point of health and strength. It was the first faint stirring of contact. The voices ran on all around. Translated sentences broke over my mind. I pressed his hand which lay, forlorn and useless, on the blanket. "You got here safely, then," he said. Perhaps it was meant ironically, perhaps not.

"And so did you... Adam came with me. He insisted on coming."

"Ah, the book man..."

The conversation petered out. We had reached a dead end. I cast about for something to say to repair the breach. But it was Jude who came to the rescue. He turned his head a fraction on the pillow. His eyes were alert now, his breathing more pronounced. He looked at me with mute entreaty. It made my heart quicken, for rarely had we been able to see eye to eye. "Angie... I *know*. I know what you were trying to tell me the night before I left. It's so clear to me... I can't recall the crash, any of it, but that night at home is so clear in my mind."

My eyes were downcast, intently tracing the veins on his hands. He raised his own to the ceiling, searching its sterile expanses. "I've been so blind," he went on. "Suddenly, it all made sense. I was in the plane coming here. It was a glorious day. I was buoyed up that all would work out for the best with Kaufmann. I could see the city from the plane. Its domes were glistening in the sun... all copper-frosted. It was beautiful... almost visionary... like... like Jerusalem... and then something you said came to me. *It's never going to get any better. There's nothing they can do.* And I knew what you meant. It all fell into place. This last year... Why you couldn't tell me..."

His fingers were twisting wretchedly around mine. "Why is it that everything good in my life turns out to be an anathema? The things I care for most dearly, when I possess them, turn to dust?"

I wanted to speak but no sound came.

"Somehow... you've always been elusive. Now I'm going to lose you. I can't let you go, Angie, I can't face the future without you! There must be some way... Tell me I'm wrong..."

"Please don't," I begged him, anxious to avoid the attention of the staff. It would have been awful to have been interrupted and sent away at that moment.

"I'm not wrong, am I?"

"No."

"Where, where shall I find forgiveness... for not *being there*? For Marnie?"

Then it came to me, the reply, dropping like manna from heaven. "In the Eucharist," I replied. "There's nothing that can't be made good at the Lord's Table."

Surprisingly, this seemed to soothe and satisfy him. "Is that why you started to go to Mass regularly?"

"Yes."

"I didn't want you to, not without me. But I didn't want to come with you."

"No."

"It's like a miracle, having you here, large as life. A presence from another world. If you can bear it, so must I. How long? How long is there left?"

"We have only today."

"To think if there hadn't been a cancellation... I was booked on a later flight, you know. But I was anxious to get back. I couldn't concentrate on the discussions with Hans Kruger. I thought if I rang you and there was no answer..."

As there wouldn't have been. The house had been empty all day.

"You were so far away."

"Yes."

"It wouldn't have happened, but I wanted to get back. I was coming home!"

"We're only human, Jude. I think any debt is already paid, don't you? ...Is it decided, the takeover?"

"The terms won't be too disagreeable, I think. Not if we take the plunge now and don't delay."

"I'm glad." I stood up and pushed the chair back against the wall. " I must go. I hope I haven't tired you too much."

A trace of colour had appeared in his face. But I could see what it cost him to talk.

"Thank you for coming. Take care," he bade. "Ask Adam to take you to the *Haus der Kunst*. You'll enjoy the pictures."

But I wanted to hasten to the Frauenkirche, pour out my gratitude and rest in the embrace of my Mother. "I'll come and see you later," I said, pressing a kiss upon his dressings.

And now the exchanges blended together, query coupled with response, unabridged understanding. The Sister, a placid-featured frau, was only too eager to discuss the fate of *Der Englander*. They were keeping Jude under observation for two or three days and then would transfer him to Edinburgh or Perth where he would be discharged in a day or two if all went well. "A tragedy. Such a waste of life," she muttered. "*Mein Gott*, not a handful of survivors. *Sechs, sieben!*"

"Yes," I said. "He has had a narrow escape, my husband." But I saw by the woman's reaction that she did not think he was out danger yet. I could not convey my unspeakable relief or claim him to be subject to other than random laws, but I was sure he would survive.

In the corridor, Adam rose to meet me, searching my expression. I was touched by his aloneness. Adam, whose image I had worn like a talisman. "How did you find him?" he asked as we penetrated the outer doors into a wash of cold air.

"I found him," I said.

We began to walk, losing ourselves in the hectic and rapacious metropolis. I asked Adam if he would mind coming with me to the Church of Our Lady. We sat in the pale, faintly echoing silence, under the gold-ribbed vaulting, and contemplated the effects of Reformation and

Renaissance. Suddenly, Adam started and made to get up, then shuffled back into the pew, recollecting himself.

"For a moment, I thought I glimpsed Elizabeth," he said.


People moved like shadows through chromatic wings in the shallow span of light between Jude's lashes. Trolley wheels turned, systems kept moving, but this was a stationary place. The word 'retrenchment' cavorted in his mind.

He thought of the wild winds of Scotland, its lowering skies and solid towns established from time immemorial, its league upon league of forsaken road winding across heath and moor, the gentle scansion of its mountains and the smell of its peat-stained burns. Scotland!

Full awareness dawned. The light deepened and broadened. His eyes opened. In the pale sky above Munich, cirrus clouds were merging to form the coastline of a new, uncharted country.

# Night

*The sword sang on the barren heath;*
*The sickle in the fruitful field*
*The sword he sang a song of death,*
*But could not make the sickle yield.*

# Night

The takeover went through and nothing could hinder the steady march of the days. After the spring rains, the streams ran clear: a green bloom came down on the glen, softening its contours and filling its spaces. The loch turned silver-blue, laying a translucence upon the dry shingle.

I went down to it often and, when he had mended, Jude came with me. Together we sat on the shore as we had years ago, when Scotland was a vision to beckon us.

When I turned to him now, I perceived that the callowness had gone from his spirit, a new strength, a wisdom, was born in its place. He was someone to lean on, his a hand to steady me over the rocks. I'd to let him do what he must, things I might well accomplish myself. I'd to let him wait upon me; it was unkind to protest, for it would help to salve the pain later when I was beyond any comfort that he could bestow. He must work it out of himself while he could. And I found it did not irk or irritate me as I had once thought. I was glad for him.


For his part, Jude saw the tranquillity flower in Angel's bearing, the straining and striving gone from her gaze and the irony lost to her voice. She no longer reminded him of a prisoner locked in a cell. *All that time, life kept putting its face around the door, but never came into the room*, she said.

He nodded pensively. Hadn't he, too, seen suns rising and setting over the mountain between his frenzied skirmishes with life?

"I've come such a long way in so short a space. A whole lifetime's span in a year or two."

"We both have."

"And the journey isn't done yet. Perhaps it never will be. I still want..."

But she could not explain what it was that she wanted, sitting there while wavelets danced over the water, satisfying a sense of expectation and rhythm, or that it was without anxiety that she wanted it. She was content. She could not tell him how precious was the tenor of these days, the zest of young heather sighing down the braes, crystal spindrift flying in the face of the sun, the lark dropping covertly to his dwelling-place; evanescent days gone like a dream, leaving in her heart a residue of sadness that exile was necessary in order to enter into belonging. One dusk they heard the nightingale and she went down to sleep with the sound of it echoing far and away beyond the temporal plane where she rested.

When they returned home, it was together, not colliding on the threshold, he going this way, she going that. They walked hand in hand, a step at a time, and his metal-rimmed heels struck sparks on the road. He quite lost the habit of vaulting fences and bounding up and down stairs four at a time. He moved over the uneven terrain, sure-footed as a goat. Part and parcel of the landscape he was, found proper clothes for their sallies, he who'd grown used to slick city suits and a plush recliner in his air-conditioned office with the intercom on his desk. He felt fitter than he had for years. His sleep was sounder, too. For, at first, he'd lain awake in suspense, listening, waiting, and thanked God when a fresh day surprised them, a new dawn pearled the sky and she opened her eyes. Despite the fate hanging over him, he'd no desire to have done with it quickly. The rift needed time to heal, he wanted to make amends. Every day was a remission from his own bad debt and he welcomed it with gratitude and wonder.

So the days rolled on and a fine savour they had. This was a brief interval from which he would have to draw strength for a very long time. He accepted that now. He'd no mind to squander it going to the ends of the earth for improbable solutions. All things were in the palm of God. Nor did he quicken his step past the churchyard or look the other way. You couldn't avoid it altogether, the house had no other approach. One night she lingered there at the lych-gate, and he did not demur. She was struck how the cruciform shapes sprang out of the earth and shone pale in the twilight, upright they grew, a plantation set in a hillside. *When the time comes,* Angel said, her face lost in the shadows, *when it comes, weep for me. Yes, I want you to weep. Bring to that hollow they will make in the ground all your anger, your bitterness and guilt. Then go away and live your life. Put the past behind you. Let the gap close up and the earth knit together so that the grass can grow green again.*

Listening to her, Jude realised it was pure common sense, not morbid at all. He thought how often the word 'despatched' was used for 'dead'. People had no contact with it. Whatever pain and sadness he endured, he would surface the richer and be happy again. The sting and the menace would go out of life, the sense of panic would be vanquished for good. He would obtain peace through trial. He would bring armfuls of flowers to her grave as a token of Resurrection.

*I see now,* he told her one night in the bedroom, after they had been discussing the takeover, *that the whole of my life has been built on false premises.*

"I wish," Angel sighed, "that you would make peace with your mother."

"I haven't crossed swords with her."

"Don't you feel betrayed?"

"I did. But not any more. The takeover was for the best. We're still an autonomous unit. We've retained our identity."

And it was true that no asperity strove in his heart. All that had dissolved in the presence of death. But the figure of his mother was remote, unreal, far out on an untouched perimeter. He saw no way of drawing her in. She was. And he was. What would be would be.

Angel reached out, glad of that, and embraced him. She understood how much he'd to bear with her gentle advice, knowledge hoarded against the day of their parting, that the minor concerns he'd taken no thought for should not defeat him. It was a giving and a taking on both sides. He was becoming daily aware of the diffuse gifts of womanhood, how the road was being constantly smoothed for his launch into the future. "Love me," she whispered. The look changed in his eye. Keen-edged it became. He had treated her like porcelain, had never approached her. How could it matter, their union? But he wanted to touch her, be close to her. For, though the estrangement between them had gone, he sometimes saw her listening to the call of that thing beyond life, felt sorely his own separateness.

So, when she had silenced his lips with her finger and dispelled all his doubts, she took him to herself and together they wept and it was not her hollowness he sounded now, but the lilt of an endless refrain. Night air lisped about the room with the scent of worn summers and those left in store while tides turned on cue and the earth went on folding generations to her breast.


It was on those days when Adam sensed Angel most poignantly, that she would materialise at the gate.

She would discover him in the garden, gauntleted, pulling the weeds with such absorption that she did not like to intrude, the time for pruning and cutting back over, the emphasis now on new growth.

"It's best to keep on top of them," he told her. "It repays a little effort. The roots weaken in time."

The sound of Mozart or Delius or Berlioz would come floating out of the house to mix with that of honeysuckle, neglected roses, worked soil. He strove for the best of all worlds, Adam.

Then he would smile, that look of penetrating amusement spreading over his features, for she had not come to hear a lecture on horticulture, had she? "It's good to see you. A tonic," he would declare. That spirit of levity and celebration would supervene. "Come in. I'll make some coffee."

They'd go in to where the music was playing. As often as not, she'd make the coffee herself, grinding the beans in an old wooden mill while he tidied a place for them to sit. The exigencies of the garden and book-world left little opportunity for attention to chores. He'd seen to it that what occupied him outside absorbed him within.

Sometimes, she would bring cakes for him, airy confections of coffee and honey and nuts, which he ate to the very last morsel, never scolding her for the trouble she'd taken, even in fun. He took and enjoyed and his pleasure was infectious. She felt so intensely *alive* in his company, sparing no thought for what lay ahead. He made no overt allowances for her ailing condition, treated her as ever he had. Their feeling for one another had undergone a transmutation, not flowing awry on a headstrong course of its own, but suffusing and enriching every area of experience. It did not matter if she did not come from one week to the next. In absence nothing was lost. When they met, there was no need to waste time picking up threads, they were off straight away on a joyous adventure, albeit spent in the garden among heather-fringed paths.

Adam knew that if it rained, Angel would not come. It was only then that he lapsed into disquiet. But fortune smiled, it seldom rained in the daytime, only fell in the dark hours, just enough to refresh the plants.

August came: starflower blue the skies. The new-mown hay was thick with clover, its dust filtering out over the countryside. Animals darted for cover elsewhere, missing the reaper's blade by a whisker's span. Heat shimmered off the walls. On his own lawn, Adam stumbled across a four-leaf clover and brought it to Angel with that same delight he had discovered the heartsease months ago.

"I heard from Elizabeth this morning," he confided. "Andrew's coming up for rest of the summer holiday next week."

Naturally, he was looking forward to it. His voice was resonant with anticipation. "You could come with us on our expeditions. We shall follow badgers' trails and hunt the eyrie of the golden eagle. Why don't you?"

She shook her head, smiling, touched.

"He'd love you, I know he would."

"No, Adam. He must have you to himself."

His silence seemed to confirm that the war of interests had been amicably resolved.

"Besides," Angel said, "I shouldn't want to be a drag, lag behind, spoil things. I haven't the strength to quest for golden eagles."

A summer fatigue had overtaken her, weariness drenching down into her bones with the sun. Where her eyes had been limpid, they were slightly opaque, as if the world and its demands was foreclosing upon her.

Maybe it was then, gazing down at the leaf, that she began to see in its irregular shape, the germination of something new. For days and days it wrestled within her, she hadn't a notion what it was or how it came to be. A sense of disorientation took hold of her, vaguely familiar, just like the old days when she didn't belong, and yet different still. The blood fizzed around her sinuses like a heady wine, forcing her head down, down to take rest. The weeks ran together. Sleep came in deep draughts. She woke, vexed, to a new day and craved only for fruit, exotic fruit, more and still more of it. Melons and pineapples, grapes, green figs, these were what slaked her feverish palate.

In the wood, along the thinning hedgerows, berries ripened in clusters of scarlet and orange and gold, blackberries bloated with amethystine juice. Folk said it would be a hard winter. No more the wheat swayed in Glenfinnie's fields. Acres of stubble gleamed coarsely under the harvest moon, the grain sifted, the stalks hacked from their roots. Fire spread over the hills. All night its acrid odour came in waves through the house. By day, the rawness and vibrance of colour appalled her. Her eyes ached with crimson, nausea rose inside her at the sight of ochres and greens. She longed for darkness and quiet, for the mists to come down and the jaded tints of winter.

Jude looked on, at a loss to help her. She refused at that point to see a doctor.

And then the phase passed, as abruptly as it had come. She was calm and settled again. Her skin which had dried out in these last few weeks, glowed clear and soft. Her eyes shone as brilliantly as ever. A kindness had come into them, deeper than humour, deeper yet than goodwill, as though every last vestige of fear and doubt had been put to flight by her mortification. It was a kind of death and new life, a shedding of husks. A going on.

At last she understood what was happening. She looked out to the hills not wishing for winter, nor yet afraid of its approach. She looked with love upon the changing face of the earth, knew herself to be of it, a limb, an adjunct.

"We must find room for the cradle," Angel told Jude. *"We're going to have a baby."*

He would never forget the peculiar triumph with which she imparted this news.

"It can't be true," he said. He slumped down on the sofa, the ground cut from under him.

"It is true."

"Have you seen the doctor?"

"Yes."

"What does he say?"

"She. They'll do all they can when the time comes. Meanwhile I'll have regular checks like everyone else. She was very kind."

"But can't they do something now? I mean, can't they...?"

"No."

"But I thought... when it endangered life... "

Tired petals fell from the last of the roses Angel had arranged in a bowl on the table.

"Don't you see, it's a miracle? Aren't you pleased? Aren't you glad?" she cajoled him, concealing her disappointment at being rebuked for her gift. Perhaps it was too much to hope that he would see it as she did.

Jude was bewildered by the new strength, the new sense of power which turned her head. It effaced him.

"If you can't consider yourself, at least consider me. Consider the child. What will become of us?"

"Oh Jude," Angel sighed. She didn't see it in that light at all. The picture was a bigger one. "I feel it was *meant*. We didn't choose it. It isn't for us to intervene."

"But how can you be so fatalistic in view of the circumstances? It doesn't make any kind of sense."

She suspected that they had trodden this ground before, the landmarks were familiar.

"If it isn't meant to be, it will come to nothing. There's a fair chance of that, they say. But I know in my bones it's going to be all right. Strength will come. For both of us."

That odd otherworld light had returned to her eyes, an inner excitement, a profound assurance he knew he could never share. What for him was no less than a tragedy, was for her a crown of blessings. For the first time he glimpsed the full meaning of her Catholic philosophy in all its fearful simple beauty. He believed he had the measure of death, but not this, this he could not reconcile. He could never surrender himself so abjectly to a Divine Will. There was too much at stake.

The following day, when she went to Mass, he stayed behind.

Adam, on the other hand, received the news rapturously. Andrew had gone back to school. He surveyed her in loving disbelief, took both her hands and swung them wide. "How you must feel," he said. "When is it to be?"

"In April. In the spring."

The *Symphonie Fantastique* was coming from the music centre, the section entitled *Un Bal* where the harp ripples free and comes into its own.

"When I was small," she reflected, "I used to dance to this. It was the most beautiful sound in the world... You're smiling. Why are you smiling your secretive smile?"

"I knew, you know. Somehow one does know these things. That's exactly how I saw you the day we first met."

"How did I see you, I wonder? Oh, but I shan't tell you!"

His shoulders were shaking with silent mirth as they did when he was unbearably happy."

"I remember when Elizabeth was expecting Andrew," he said, the reference so natural she might merely have gone to answer the doorbell, "we would sit in the evenings listening to this. This and Chopin."

The passage that followed *Un Bal* was sheer torment, Angel knew. It seemed to have little connection with what came before, a fugitive enchantment spun out of suffering. *I can't bear it,* she thought. *I can't bear to be severed from this.* It was late afternoon. They sky was fading to a watery green, sombre-streaked with cloud. Birches quivered in the glen like armies of spectral gold, frail spiritual things. *I shan't ever forget you, Angel,* Adam said. For he could tell her the truth, he need not spare her. Though the presage of winter overshadowed the day, he could enter her joy at the slowly burgeoning evidence of new creation.

And so it was that the strains of the old days were taken up again, woven into a new theme, what was good and true carried over, what was depleted dying a death as surely as the leaves drifting down to moulder and reconstitute the earth.


Weeks passed and she did not come. A biting chill came down on Glenfinnie's days. Its streets were less populated; business relapsed. Folk huddled around fires and remembered. Curiously, Adam felt closer than ever to Angel now when she could not venture so far, the burden of new life expanding within her so that she grew tired before day had scarcely begun. In absence a subtle change was taking place, a deepening instinctive knowledge of her, touching on all facets of his ever-developing self. On several occasions, he went up to the house, takings flowers and books, but he did not stay long. Often Jude was there and would answer the door. "Come on in, man. Sit down. Have a drink. Not for nothing did we come to the land of pure malt Scotch!"

Angel did not care for the mask of irony with which he was lately braving his days. He was restless. His life lacked cohesion. He would go about tidying magazines, papers, clothes, putting everything in its place only to meet fresh disorder hours later. His hours of work were erratic, not entirely on Angel's account. *There are complications,* he told them at Harmony. *I have to look after her.* It was a true enough alibi. As day by precarious day went by, he began to wonder whether she was right. Perhaps there was an inscrutable purpose in the life that was coming. *What,* he even suggested, *if this were the very means of effecting a cure?* She vouchsafed no reply to that, only studied him wistfully.

Adam went away deeply distressed. She ought not to be there where she did not belong, in that place at this hour. It was all wrong. He would have taken her into his own cramped dwelling and looked after her if he could. Alone, in his home, in stillness and quietness, his heart reached out to touch her and at five to three or twenty past seven, her gaze would lift to the clock, seconds plucked out of time, and she would feel the communion.

The child thrust and struggled under her heart, its head slowly turning to enter the world. Sometimes Angel would suffer long spells of vertigo, as though a panoramic view were being thrust under her nose. Gravity bore her down, but if she kept her chin high, it was not so bad. The will burned tenaciously within her. An almost mystic light shone from her eyes.

By the seventh month she was confined to bed but adamantly refused to go into hospital.

And now the world began to draw in. The mountains gathered round her, cold as iron. Snow lay like chalk dust in the furrows at their summits, the heather gone to rust down below. Gulls wheeled and swooped over the loch flecked with crests of foam. *It was a wonderful summer, wasn't it?* she said.

In March snow fell thick and fast. Mesmerised she watched it tumble from the sky just as it had over twenty years ago, coming so late in the season, unforecast. The two incidents formed a circle in her mind, a beginning and an end linked together. Soon she was looking out on a black and white realm where no part was played by the inventions of colour. It was startling, beautiful, sending a wash of light across the bedroom walls. A magpie settled on a nearby branch and cast a scavenging eye over the frozen desert.

For days and nights the snow continued to fall, inch upon inch accruing in silence. There was nothing to compare with it in living memory. Glenfinnie town stood lapped in white dunes, lost to the rest of civilisation; some said it was no bad thing! Passes were blocked, journeys halted in motion, vehicles and sheep trapped beneath drifts. Angel wept for the bleating of motherless lambs, stranded out in the cold on the hillside.

So while snowploughs endeavoured to carve a way through from the outside world and a special snow-blower was borrowed from Switzerland, folk shook their heads and fell back on their own resources, too occupied to worry about the next move or to press claims for damage.

At last the sky thinned to a watercolour blue. Mild currents of air swept through the glen. Icicles dripped their pellucid substance away. A thaw set in, the snow perished, the waters broke.

The pain came.


"They're on the way now. They'll be here in half an hour. Sooner," Jude called to me from the extension. He came into the room, his eyes bright with suppressed alarm. The time had come, the watching and waiting and listening done. Apart from the doctor and midwife, a nun was coming from the Convent of the Sacred Heart where I attended Mass.

Outside it was chill and damp. The grass was sun-starved and lustreless, evoking memories of Norway as it had appeared on our honeymoon several springs ago. Ah, the impenetrable mountains, the impassable roads in the long winter season. How Jude had marvelled that the natives should choose to stay.

Pain lunged at my body afresh. I caught at the bedclothes and strangled a cry. By the time help arrived, a slow paralysis was creeping along my spine. Reluctantly, they'd agreed to attend me at home, aided by the ministrations of Sister Raphael, and had rigged up a glucose drip to sustain me, the colourless fluid flowing into a punctured vein at my wrist. I had tried to explain that the gravest danger of all was to be out of context. I could not be torn from my home, from my hills, in the teeth of such a momentous event. I knew every inch of the landscape, embedded here as I had been these last few months, every crest, every crag, the long slow escarpment.

Where I went in the following hours, I don't know. The world flung itself at me and receded in waves. My spine was a lurid blade of pain, diminishing even the throes which wrung the breath from me. I thought of the swords that would be beaten into ploughshares, the spears into pruning hooks, but no longer believed it. For what could be gleaned from a land so stained and corrupted by bloodshot mists? All that mattered was that the child should be delivered. I gripped Jude's hand, pitting my failing strength against his while Sister Raphael mopped my brow, her lips moving quietly as she fingered her rosary. The doctor went. The midwife was replaced by another, all smiling energy. The doctor returned. There were whispered confabulations in corners. They were plotting to intervene.

I wanted to cry out: *No! No! Let him come of his own accord!* But I hadn't the strength. I was drained through and through. There was nowhere to rest and the journey would not come to an end. It was the narrowness that was the trouble, with the child full-term. It had always been the trouble, the constriction of apertures, the needle's eye. They cast one another looks of furtive alarm while they murmured blandishments to distract me. The sound of their voices came down a long tunnel. And then, suddenly, it changed. The way opened up. Warm blood coursed away. Cold metal ground distantly into my flesh. I rose up on a crest of pain and gave way at last. It was finished.

A protesting cry filled the room, a cry I knew and recognised down ages long, unlike the cries of other infants. *You've a daughter,* they exclaimed, their faces beaming with joy. *A broth of a bairn,* the doctor confirmed. The baby was plump and perfectly formed as a doll.

I turned to Jude then and all the roads we had travelled, the deserts traversed, all the sights we had seen, had been for this, a new generation.

Chiara Mary Brightman blinked in bemusement and yawned into my adoring gaze. It had been touch-and-go, a hazardous journey.


I drifted between sleep and a vivid awareness, my absolution complete. The gaps were closing, the revolution complete, the link forged. The cord cut. What was happening felt *right*, even safe, deeply familiar. My mother had abandoned me, and I was destined to abandon Chiara, though not from choice. But what is choice except some illusory coping mechanism?

People were still coming and going. Jude was there, his mother, too, bending over the wicker cradle brought down from the attic. Sister Raphael went out to make tea for them.

"Look after our beautiful daughter," I whispered. "Tell her..." I touched a hand to the tears trickling down Jude's face, his skin tissue-thin from the ordeal. "Tell her...'*Next year in Jerusalem*'."

"Angie… Don't leave…*us*. Hang in!"

He could barely countenance my tacit response. *And now I am going where you cannot come. But I shall guard you and pray for you, make a home for you, that where I am you may be also.*

When Sister Raphael returned bearing a tray, she was not alone. She had let in a visitor. I cannot say I was startled by the woman, for I was consumed with a blissful expectancy, though her beauty was of an unearthly order. The very air she moved through shone with a kind of resonance.

"Who…? At this hour?"

Jude must have been taken aback, else he did not hear, for he uttered no response.

The woman's beatific smile drew me to her heart. It filled me with joy and an exquisite lightness of limb. My stitches ceased to smart; my leaden frame to dissolve. I was strong again. Music poured through my being. I could dance! I rose from the bed to be engulfed in her embrace. "Oh!"

"I'm going with her," I said. "You must understand… There's a lot of catching up to do."

But Jude remained corpse-still with yearning to reanimate that effigy I once was in the dead land.


The atmosphere in the room was electric. The short hand of the travelling clock by the bedside, pointing straight up, was eclipsed by the long hand. For several seconds it seemed poised on the cusp of midnight before it inclined to the other side. The child stirred and murmured, but did not wake, her miniature fingers groping on air.

There was life on the one hand and death on the other and he, Jude, pinioned midway between. Where had he come from and where was he going?

Far away a tortured cry broke the spell, the howl of an animal trapped in a snare. And he remembered the darkness beyond the bounds of these walls, that it was still night out there. There was sleep to be had and work to be done. Life had to move on. The cycle was beginning all over again and he was a captive of motion.

No word of her came, not a whisper for days. No news, Adam supposed, was the best news.

Except that one morning he woke very early, well before the alarm went off. Tangled dreams steered close to the surface of thought. His ribs ached as though from excessive strain. He couldn't think what he had done to produce it.

Nothing ran smoothly that day. His tasks would not integrate for all the effort he spent. The sky was like unwritten parchment. Not a breath of wind stirred the nerve-ends of the trees, knotted with bursting buds. The world waited on the brink of revelation. At any moment the light would break through and come pouring from the cloud.

When he could stand the tension no longer, he put on his coat and went out through the garden where many of the new bulbs lay crushed and battered from the weather. The gate swung on its hinges.

But even by the loch, there was no comfort to be had. He had blundered into a placid, upturned world without motion or relief, simply areas of shadow and a faint feathering upon the water, the mountains lost and unwrought behind fog. He stooped and picked up a stone, cold to his touch, flung it in a wide arc over the loch, watching the ripples spread out to the circumference of pain. "Oh God!" he cried hoarsely. "Why?" A frail tide washed at his feet and rebounded upon itself, shivering back upon the water until the calm was remade.

As evening closed in, the weather changed. He sat up late, listening to music, and did not hear a fresh wind blow or see the night broadcast with stars. At midnight, almost exactly, the rapturous interlude from the *Symphonie Fantastique* gathered up its essence and poured into the room, the theme she had danced to in long ago childhood. A draught swelled the curtain. The power of that chaos and madness which had imprisoned him all day was broken. He wasn't alone. The whole room, the whole house was full of her.

Adam wept.


The following day was bright and clear, the flash of white wings soaring above, vapour trails intersecting in a naked sky. In the garden new blades of green were pushing up from the soil. Adam bent down and began to turn over the earth lightly with a trowel to let in the air. Lime-veined ivy rustled on the wall, burnished to a brilliant sheen.

A presence whispered about the unborn foliage. Out of habit, out of longing, he looked up.

Elizabeth stood at the open gate.

www.ingramcontent.com/pod-product-compliance
Lightning Source LLC
Chambersburg PA
CBHW031348170626
46807CB00002B/865